Amanda Calderon

KANISHK THAROOR's writing has appeared in *The New York Times, The Guardian, VQR,* and elsewhere. His short story "Tale of the Teahouse" was nominated for a National Magazine Award. He is the presenter of the BBC radio series *Museum of Lost Objects*. Born in Singapore, and raised in Geneva, Kolkata, and New York, he now lives with his wife in Brooklyn.

Additional Praise for

SWIMMER AMONG THE STARS

"[A] remarkably crafted and imaginative debut . . . If it's true, as is said in 'The Loss of Muzaffar,' that 'humanity, after all, was nothing but a library,' then the experience of reading this collection is like watching a contemplative, concerned—yet playful—observer leafing through its volumes."

—Meron Hadero, *The New York Times Book Review*

"Sparkling, magical, heartbreaking . . . Whimsical and wise . . . Graceful, haunting . . . It's a testament to the author's empathy, rich voice, and immaculate craftsmanship that [*Swimmer Among the Stars*] succeeds in being all these things—even as it comforts, illuminates, and unnerves."

—Jason Heller, NPR

"You can open *Swimmer Among the Stars* to any page and find a sentence worth quoting, a scenario worth remembering. Though the stories span the Battle of Magnesia, in which Rome defeated the Seleucid Empire, to a dystopian future in which the United Nations has been chased to a near-Earth orbit, Tharoor wears his erudition lightly, privileging poetry over political messaging. Lush, playful, and intoxicated by history, the book stuck with me long after I closed it."

—David Busis, *Electric Literature*

"It's the details within the details that get me—there's just this beautiful telescoping the writing does between a kind of ruthless precision and something just as close up but more tender, like counting fingers and toes."

—Helen Oyeyemi

"A virtuoso debut collection that is as globalist as it is fabulist."

—*O, The Oprah Magazine*

"Cosmopolitan in its approaching the world as one large village with many shared narratives, this collection reminds us of all that we have in common, even as we demarcate our differences with walls and borders. Tharoor writes with a clarity that expresses his insights into characters and contexts, ultimately attaining a striking lushness." —Shoba Viswanathan, *Booklist*

"Tharoor is clearly a monumental talent, and his debut is a pleasure, from the first page to the last."

—*Kirkus Reviews* (starred review)

"Tharoor's collection is imaginative and relevant."

—*Publishers Weekly*

"It's been years since I've encountered a collection as beguiling as *Swimmer Among the Stars*. Kanishk Tharoor seems to have sprung onto the scene fully formed, possessed of his own mischievous and erudite voice, already at the full height of his powers. Literary debuts are often described as 'promising'; here are stories that read like promises fulfilled." —John Wray

"Like the storytellers of old, as well as the art's twentieth-century masters, Kanishk Tharoor brings together times past and our present day in his dazzling fables where the exotic and the mundane, the lost and the hoped for, are woven into images that remind the reader that it is through sharing stories, and maybe stories alone, that civilizations and their subjects come together in surviving whatever tasks history sets for them." —Sjón

"These stories gleam with the light of an authentic and wholly original imagination, beautifully crafted and in possession of an untamed, almost feral sense of creativity. With Borgesian intelligence and great tenderness of heart, Tharoor reminds us how vital it is to tell stories, and how urgently we need to consume them." —Alexandra Kleeman, author of *You Too Can Have a Body Like Mine*

"His writing has the clarity and expansiveness of fable."
—*The Sunday Times* (London)

"A highly playful and imaginative collection."
—*Financial Times*

SWIMMER AMONG THE STARS

STORIES

KANISHK THAROOR

PICADOR FARRAR, STRAUS AND GIROUX NEW YORK

These are works of fiction. All of the characters, organizations, and events portrayed in these stories are either products of the author's imagination or are used fictitiously.

picadorusa.com • instagram.com/picador
twitter.com/picadorusa • facebook.com/picadorusa

Picador® is a U.S. registered trademark and is used by Macmillan Publishing Group, LLC, under license from Pan Books Limited.

For book club information, please visit facebook.com/picadorbookclub or email marketing@picadorusa.com.

These stories previously appeared, in slightly different form, in the following publications: *VQR* ("Tale of the Teahouse"), *A Clutch of Indian Masterpieces* ("Elephant at Sea"), *First Proof* ("The Loss of Muzaffar"), and *Scroll.in* ("The Fall of an Eyelash").

Designed by Jo Anne Metsch

The Library of Congress has cataloged the Farrar, Straus and Giroux edition as follows:

Names: Tharoor, Kanishk, author.
Title: Swimmer among the stars : stories / Kanishk Tharoor.
Description: First American edition. | New York : Farrar, Straus and Giroux, 2017.
Identifiers: LCCN 2016025615 | ISBN 9780374272180 (hardcover) | ISBN 9780374715397 (ebook)
Subjects: | BISAC: FICTION / Literary.
Classification: LCC PS3620.H348 A6 2017 | DDC 813'.6—dc23
LC record available at https://lccn.loc.gov/2016025615

Picador Paperback ISBN 978-1-250-16012-6

Our books may be purchased in bulk for promotional, educational, or business use. Please contact your local bookseller or the Macmillan Corporate and Premium Sales Department at 1-800-221-7945, extension 5442, or by email at MacmillanSpecialMarkets@macmillan.com.

Originally published, in slightly different form, in India by Aleph Book Company

First published in the United States by Farrar, Straus and Giroux

First Picador Edition: March 2018

10 9 8 7 6 5 4 3 2 1

To Ma, Daddy, Ishaan, and Amanda

Arriving at each new city, the traveler finds again a past of his that he did not know he had: the foreignness of what you no longer are or no longer possess lies in wait for you in foreign, unpossessed places.

—ITALO CALVINO, *Invisible Cities*

CONTENTS

SWIMMER AMONG THE STARS

As a rule, the last speaker of a language no longer uses it. Ethnographers show up at the door with digital recorders, ready to archive every declension, each instance of the genitive, the idiosyncratic function of verbal suffixes. But this display hardly counts as normal speech. It simply confirms reality to the last speaker, that the old world of her mind is cut adrift from humans and can only be pulped into a computer. She finds it strange to listen to the sounds of her mouth. Inevitably, she mingles a more common language with her own. That common language, after all, is the speech that now keeps her company, that leads her through the market, that sits with her in the evenings by the television, that gives her the terminal diagnosis at the clinic, that pours through her letterbox, that comes in a crisp nurse's outfit to wash her feet. Her own language does nothing of the sort. It is nowhere to be found. She pauses, silent now, staring incredulously at the microphone. How am I the last speaker of my language? How can I be its keeper? My language left me.

She apologizes to the ethnographers. You must understand, she says, that though my memory is preserved better than a lemon, it is still difficult to remember which words are my own and which words are not.

Please speak as it comes naturally to you, the ethnographers say.

Thank you, I will try.

In any case, we can help you remember.

The last speaker looks up, puzzled. But if you know already, then why do you want to hear it from me?

It means something more if it comes from you.

Do you speak my language then? Do you understand me when I say this, when I say that, and even now, when I am singing this song that my father sang every day as he disappeared down the valley? She sings and her alien words crackle about the room.

No, we do not understand, the ethnographers say. Or if we do, it is only distantly.

Oh, that is a shame, it would be nice to sing that song for someone.

Please, madam, sing it for the microphone.

She grins. So the microphone understands, does it?

Yes, it understands.

If only you could get microphones to talk! She laughs and then feels a little sorry for herself. She does not mean to sound sardonic; no one could accuse her of being indifferent to her plight. Some years before, it had occurred to her that she was no longer in the habit of hearing her own tongue. Everybody in the town seemed to be speaking the common language. She did not mind using their language, since she had dwelled in it for a long time, almost as long as she could remember, and had kept it clean and given it a good airing, rearranged the furniture so it suited her just right. It was the language of her husband and her children, and she had made it hers. But always, in the darker corners, she placed mementos of her own, a proverb, a snatch of a rhyme, some light daily expressions the glimpse of which would startle her family. With nobody to speak her language to, she began talking with objects, the pots and pans, a creaking door, the sharp corner of a table. She never spoke it with animals because—and here a foreign kind of pride sparked within her—it was never a language to waste on goats. Once, on a rare visit, her son came upon her in the living room, speaking with a teacup. He told her she was going mad. No, she sighed, you don't understand, this is what a conversation sounds like.

Would you like a cup of tea? the last speaker asks the ethnographers. They would. Let's have some tea and then I'll sing for you. She rises from her seat and waits as they shift their equipment, the light stand and camera, the microphones, the attendant knots of wires. Brushing away their offers to assist her, she lights the stove with a match and stares out through the kitchen window. Poplars nod in the breeze over the mustard field. Someone's boy is loitering at the front gate, his hands in the pockets of his jeans. At each half-step, his sneakers light up red. She thinks he must be here to look at the visitors, but she is wrong. He follows her movements with open curiosity, as if there was something surprising about the way a kettle boils. She smiles: that's the matter with strange guests, they turn you into a stranger as well.

The tea warms her voice. When she sings, her eyes close and her chin with its gentle down of hair thrusts forward into the lamplight. The ethnographers cannot help but admire her strong set of teeth, a rare sight in so much of their work. They are used to thinking that there is half a relationship between dental health and endangered languages; languages, like people, become toothless. In her case, of course, a full mouth of teeth won't make any difference. She is the last, the very last. After her, the language has only a ghostly future. Few even remember the time when its clambering rhythms united the valley and the uplands. Clinically speaking, it is already dead. A language cannot be alive if it exists alone in the mind of an old woman, no matter how fine her teeth.

The song is about a wedding. At the end of the festivities, the bride leads the groom out from the town, through the fields and up the slope of a mountain. Where will it happen? the groom asks. The bride kisses him and beckons him to follow. He does. She allows him another kiss after a hundred steps, and another after another hundred, and so on until they can walk no farther and are forced to start climbing. Perturbed, the groom grabs her wrist: Why not here? She shakes her head and slips out of his grasp, removing a scarf and draping it over his shoulder. She hoists herself up the face of the mountain. The groom can see the stars shining through her hair. As they climb, she leaves bits of clothing and jewelry for him to gather: bangles, her belt, a necklace, a vest, socks. When he reaches the top, he finds her naked and motionless. Only when he touches her does he realize that she has turned to stone.

The last speaker stops. She apologizes again. Our songs are sad songs. Nobody ever gets to have sex.

The ethnographers smile vaguely. Even the most capable among them can understand at most a handful of her words, an occasional phrase. The full meaning of the song awaits its patient digestion in a computer lab. For now, their responsibility is only to the collection of raw material and the husbanding of its source, a happy task. They are growing fond of the last speaker, softened by her unabashed, tuneless singing. Privately, they all feel the stirrings of great affection, the sort that civilians might call sympathy but they know to be truer still, the love of the student for the studied.

Can I sing it again? the last speaker asks. I would like to change the ending.

By all means, they say, whenever you are ready. The ethnographers, after all, are modern enough to know that nothing can be totally genuine. Traditions are invented to be reinvented. If the last speaker wants to sex up a folk song, so be it. In any case, it's the form of the words that matters, the syntax and structure of her speech. Everything else is just pleasant air.

This song departs entirely from the previous version, but the ethnographers cannot sense the fullness of the difference, nor can they tell that she is improvising fresh phrases. The bride eludes the groom and disappears from the wedding festivities. She journeys to the mountain. At its summit, she finds a rocket (here, the last speaker pauses to construct a suitable compound for the noun "rocket," which she renders with verbal suffixes as "fiery flight in void into void"). The bride enters and speeds up to the heavens. Everything recedes beneath her. The bride has never wanted to be a bride, but rather an astronaut ("swimmer among the stars"), and fair enough, why should brides be brides when they can be astronauts? In space, the astronaut dances between satellites ("invisible lightning moths") and befriends the moon. They drink wine and watch TV ("chaos of shadows in stillness") together. The sun grows jealous, since the moon is its bride. It asks mankind to fetch the astronaut back: Why do you let her be up there? If your women become astronauts, who will be your brides? Mankind agrees: this is a worrying situation. The prime minister ("temporary rent-collector") is sent to the moon to reason with her. He sets up a table on the surface and waits for her to appear for negotiations. He waits and waits, not knowing that the moon has whisked the astronaut to its dark side. The vastness of space inspires only a deep resignation in him. But he has a mission to fulfill, so he remains seated on the surface of the moon, facing an empty chair, expecting a woman who will never come.

Look what I've done, the last speaker says after finishing. I'm such an old fool, I haven't changed the ending at all.

The ethnographers chuckle. There's no sex this time either?

Not a drop, she says, not a drop. She falls silent, her face sinking. The ethnographers think she must be tired—it is always a little unfair to bustle into the homes of lonely pensioners and force them to talk. Indeed, the last speaker is tired, but not from the physical exertion of speech. If anything, inventing within her language is invigorating. Why haven't I done this before? she wonders. Why haven't I made with my language?

But another realization exhausts her: there is no simple direct way in her language to express the idea of a "tractor." Perhaps there was a time long ago, before she was born, when her language could tackle all concepts of the fields and towns, when it was large enough to be its own world. In her life, it has only ever been in retreat. She grew up hearing it at home, in the living room and around the stoves and in the whispering dark of the bedroom she shared with her sisters. At school, they made her speak the common language. The teachers slapped her wrists if she ever misspoke and emitted the unwelcome sounds of her own tongue. As she grew older, the living room was overtaken by the radio, then the TV. She lost her bedroom and gained her husband's. The language survived a little while longer in the kitchen, nourished by the memory of food. Then her sisters passed away. For most of her life, funerals were the only occasions she would hear her language outside the home. Now there is no one else left to die. When it comes time for her funeral, she will be remembered by common people, in common words, with common ideas.

One way to represent "tractor," she thinks, could be "making absence of presence," the way a tractor levels a field with its roaring bulk, but surely that is a bit vague. "Tilling with power of many men" seems too literal and inelegant for her liking. Piling on the suffixes to a verb, she settles on an image, "smoke mowing through grass." That might do for "tractor," but this is an impossible task. She looks at all the equipment brought by the ethnographers. Her language has no natural way of referring to a camera, a microphone, a digital recorder. It has been in exile from this world, and so it is no longer of this world. She could come up with phrases for all these objects, but what would be the point? No matter how innovative she is with her language, it does not have the force to take possession of an idea. In later years, they will say that her term "swimmer among the stars" means "astronaut." They will never say that "astronaut" means "swimmer among the stars."

Have you done this before? she asks the ethnographers. Have you listened to other old women sing?

Yes, they say, but none sing as magically as you.

You shouldn't flatter me. The ancient know their weaknesses better than anybody else.

When you are rested, we'd be happy to record more of your songs.

I don't need to rest. What do you do with these recordings? Where do they go? Who listens to them?

We'll take them to our university, the ethnographers say, we'll study them, we'll write about them, we'll archive them. We'll organize them such that all future generations can learn about you and your language.

It must get noisy over there, with all those voices of old people trying to make themselves heard. She laughs. She knows how computers work, how she can be skimmed into light, vanished into the whirring density of a hard drive. That's what will happen to me, she thinks, what a drab afterlife. Technology can be so deadening. She worries sometimes that in the future all language will disappear, never mind just her own. When her grandchildren visit, they strew themselves about the house and play games on their little black phones. If they speak to each other, it is in timid bits of sound she does not understand.

What are the ethnographers making, this archive of languages? She imagines a cavernous exhibition hall, its walls lined with screens. Old women and men stare out of each one, speaking their lonely languages in an unending loop. During the day, visitors come to marvel at the spectacle of so many lost tongues. Inevitably, they feel sad and perhaps light candles or leave flowers, as if they were at a mausoleum. The figures in the screens wait patiently for the visitors to leave. At night, after hours, they interrupt their own digitized soliloquies, listen to one another, and laugh at all the jokes.

Where is your university? she asks.

In our country, very far away from here.

She squints at them and makes no attempt to veil her disappointment. Why didn't you take me there? It would be much easier. When you do this again, fetch the next old woman to your university. All of you wouldn't have had to go through this hassle or had to bring your van into our narrow streets. I would have gotten to see your country. Maybe I would have even recorded the way your people speak. Then, I could return home with your words and study you!

The ethnographers look at each other. In our work, they say a little hesitantly, it's best to talk to our informants in their native surroundings. In any case, we were worried about your health, we weren't sure if you would cope with the rigors of travel.

She straightens. I'm well aware that I'm on my way. It makes no difference to me where I die, in this chair, or on a plane, or in your university.

Why don't we let you rest for a bit? The ethnographers feel wretched for making her morose.

No, no. She waves them away. You're not tiring me. It's just . . . until you came, I never thought of my language as a burden, but that's what it is, isn't it? You want to take it from me so I no longer have to carry this weight.

It should not be just yours to bear.

Will you do me this favor? Whatever recordings you make of me speaking my language in the coming days, please put together a little package and have it played at my funeral ceremony.

The ethnographers want to hold her. Their words seem to come through a mist. We can do that, they say.

I'm much obliged to you, she says, I'm very grateful that you have come here to see me and let me feel old in my language. She means it, too—to whom else can she pass this inheritance? Her children may have known a handful of words when they were young, but their mother's tongue was always too much of a responsibility. They would come home from the fields or the houses of their friends or from school and look at their mother with a kind of fatigue, as if her language was only another chore, as tedious as dishes. She thought about making a more concerted effort to teach them, but where could she begin? As far as she knew, her language was not something that was ever taught. How could she explain its quixotic use of tenses, its habit of piling on suffixes to verbs, its wealth of nouns, when she had no knowledge of all that herself? Her ability was only intuitive, the work of habit, not understanding. In their classrooms, her children would go to the blackboard and write out conjugations in the common language. They memorized ditties that helped explain the subjunctive and mnemonics that guided correct spelling. Against this ordered system of rules, her own language seemed amorphous, entirely shapeless. What was allowed and what wasn't? she wondered. When her father sang his songs or when her sisters gossiped about the grocer in front of him, could it be that in speaking they had often misspoken? She didn't begrudge the fact that her children eventually shed what language she had given them. How could they know that the babble of their mother was a language at all?

Her son now farms in his wife's town on the other side of the valley, not far, but far away enough that he does not see his mother often. Her daughter was always the cleverer of the two, destined for the city and its indispensable comforts: air-conditioning, coffee, the admiring glances of strangers. Every month, her daughter sends her some money. They speak often on the phone, and their conversations are loving and repetitive, as all loving conversations should be. She is proud that neither of her children is vulnerable to false nostalgia, that they find full satisfaction in the present of their lives.

In my language, she tells the ethnographers, words for gratitude are much different than in the common speech. We have many kinds. This, for instance, is used to express a very dark kind of gratitude, to be thankful for the loss of something. This means to be grateful despite yourself, with a hint of bitterness. This is used to describe a sudden, overwhelming feeling of gratitude. This is the feeling children have when they receive small treats, like sweets, or when they are lifted by an adult and spun and spun.

The ethnographers take notes. Nobody ever compiled a complete grammar or lexicon of the language, so part of their mission is to attempt to reconstruct the language in its fullness. They will never know that in her language there were more than a dozen ways of indicating and describing gratitude. Here are a few more: the gratitude of natural things for one another, like the hive for the branch, the tree for the bees, the cloud for the sun; collective gratitude, the thanks of a family or a town or a people; gratitude—directed to the cosmos—for superiority, for knowing that one is better than everybody else; the gratitude of one saved from death by starvation.

Her language boasted many verbs for which no simple equivalents exist in the common language. For example, this means to be afraid of seeing time pass. This means to tell stories in the depths of winter. This is the action of stirring a kind of gravy in a pot; this also denotes the motion of a pig rooting around in the mud. This refers to the way light splinters against a range of mountains at dusk. This describes in one word how mountains gain mass and shape at dawn. This means to feel strange in an unfamiliar place. This means to be patient for spring. As does this. And this.

If she remembered all or some of these words, the last speaker's testimony would be a little more refined. Unfortunately, she doesn't remember them. Some she never knew in the first place. It's not her fault, no measure of her intelligence or sophistication. When the number of speakers of a language shrinks, so does the language itself. She grew up with an impoverished vocabulary, a skulking tongue, never with the means to recover those lost words. The ethnographers, despite their best efforts, won't be able to restore her language. How can anybody learn that which has never been written down, that which nobody knows any longer? It is sad, but sad in an unremarkable way. Humans always lose more history than they ever possess.

Speech, however, can be added to, no matter its condition. When she cannot find the word she wants in her language, she builds compounds with the words she does have. Occasionally, she imports one from the common language. She sketches her life for the ethnographers, narrates in her language the sequence of events and relationships that brought her to this chair before their camera and its severe lamp. Our father raised us in my mother's absence, which means that we raised ourselves, because he was away during the days, and often for many nights. He would come back with new clothes and boxes of contraband goods—electric fans, flyswatters, medicines, beer, and so on—that he would then shift along. (In his childhood, there was no border on the other side of the valley. I would ask him, why do you have to go over there all the time? Oh, I'm not going far, he would say, laughing, before reminding me that when he was young, over "there" was still "here." He would say that in the common language, because in our language the word for "here" is the same as the word for "there.") My favorite thing to do in the summers was to wade into the irrigation channels and feel the chill of the mountain water on my ankles. I don't remember anything from my wedding night, I got very drunk. Neither of my children likes eating cake, which is a real pity; life isn't complete without confectionery. The army installed solar ("fed by sun") streetlamps—look, they just came on!—in the village so now it's never dark at nighttime in the way our nights were once so totally dark. I miss that darkness, I miss angling lanterns and torches around corners. I only recently learned that I was the last. I had assumed there were others elsewhere, just not where I was, not here.

A neighbor interrupts the recording with a platter of pastries, a generous pretense with which to inspect the visitors. The ethnographers are ravenous. For a few moments, the sounds of grateful munching overwhelm conversation. The neighbor studies the ethnographers and their equipment, and then, for a long while, her. How quickly something familiar becomes strange when it takes shape in another language. He makes his excuses and leaves. At the door, he passes the loitering boy, who is still poking about on the threshold. The last speaker beckons to the boy. Why don't you come in? The boy shakes his head, backs a few steps away, and stares.

It is getting late. Stray dogs growl in the dust. Bicycles rustle down paths. The most popular soap operas blare from the televisions in nearby houses, where families assemble for dinner in the glow. My nurse will be coming soon, the last speaker reminds the ethnographers, and she will want to settle me for my bedtime. She won't be happy that I've strained myself like this.

Oh no! they protest. You should have allowed us to give you a break.

That's all right, I'm beginning to enjoy myself. It's coming back to me. Tomorrow, I hope I'll be able to tell you even more.

We'll return after breakfast. In fact, we'll return *with* breakfast.

How sweet, but don't go just yet. I'll sing you one more song today. Make certain your recorders are working, are they properly plugged in? Are you sure? I want a snatch of my singing played at my funeral, too.

Eager to please her, the ethnographers vigorously double-check all the controls and settings before signaling to begin. She sings, tuneless and a bit rasping, but still full.

On their wedding night, the bride and the groom retreat to the chamber prepared for them. He undresses and rushes to get under the covers. Awaiting her arrival in the pregnant darkness (a rough translation of one of many kinds of darkness in the last speaker's language), he realizes that he has not heard her talk at any point during the day. She must be shy, he thinks, she must be as nervous as I am about this moment. Is she? He feels her weight on the bed, her fingers now on his shoulder, her knee in the space between his knees. Her face looms above him, all light concentrated in the teeth. He moves to bring her mouth to his, but she pushes away and raises her torso, her hands firmly on his neck and chest, straddling him.

The last speaker stops. Thinking that she is done, the ethnographers start to commend her singing and to turn their thoughts toward dinner. She has not finished. Her eyes search the camera lens. She sings again, not quite song, more like an incantation urgent in its rhythm, her feet tapping a measure on the floor. The ethnographers strain to discern the sequence in the flow of words. Weeks later, in the computer lab, they will discover that there is no order at all in this passage. It is merely a list of unconnected phrases, shards of speech, jagged and inscrutable, the debris of a language swept clean. But in the moment, in her living room, it rises in pitch and volume and dissolves the ethnographers' scholarly attention. They surrender to the unlikely beauty of it. She looks up when she finishes. Was the song racier this time? the ethnographers grin. Was there sex? She smiles, exhausted.

Her nurse enters and looks balefully upon the scene. I'm afraid your interviews are over for the day, the nurse says, it's time for me to take care of her. The ethnographers pack away their things. They linger at the door, watching the last speaker as she settles into an armchair, puts up her feet, and turns on the TV. Until tomorrow, they say.

Until tomorrow, she replies, staring closely at the buttons on the remote. The ethnographers sputter away in their van. While the last speaker watches TV, her nurse does all the required nursely duties, checking blood pressure and temperature, feeding her the nightly quota of pills, talking to her about the antics of celebrities she only pretends to recognize. Restless, the last speaker eventually goes to the kitchen and insists on preparing dinner for both of them. What is the point of living if I can't exert myself? The nurse, who knows this routine well, protests and then acquiesces, expressing her earnest, simple gratitude. While the last speaker cooks, the nurse sinks into the armchair and starts to channel surf on the TV.

The last speaker turns to the stove. The pots begin to murmur. She whispers in her language to a smattering of onions and garlic and greens and lentils: Soon you'll become delicious and then, I'm afraid, I'm going to eat you . . . Don't worry, there's much more of you where you came from. Through her kitchen window, the wheezing solar lamps cast a light gloom over the village. She is surprised to see a hunched form sitting on her courtyard wall. It is the boy from earlier. He's been here the entire time, she thinks. Whose son is he? At her gaze, he drops from the wall and runs down the village path, red flashes in the dark, leaving her wondering if there was ever a time when she knew his name.

TALE OF THE TEAHOUSE

Seven days before the khan's army razed the city, judges presided over their courts, babies were breast-fed, the teahouse clattered with cups emptied and smashed, puppeteers led shadows through the alleyways, men and women made love, and the hum of schoolboys repeating their lessons echoed from the marble-and-granite schools. The bakeries pumped out bread and beggars woke up for yet another day of yellowed nails and coins, as if nothing at all would ever happen.

Six days before the khan's army razed the city, men and women were making love, especially the captain of the city guard, who squatted his girl on the parapets. Bored, the guards below toyed with the returning merchant caravans, skimming something—a bolt of silk, a barrel of wine, a crate of dates—off the top. The business of the city was business. Off duty, the guards sneaked to the market to hawk their loot, and then took their earnings to the brothels, from which prostitutes took their money to the bakeries, from which the pastry makers went to the butchers, who in turn visited the vegetable sellers, who shared the bloody passions of the cockfighters, who loved nothing more than long conversations with librarians, who tickled the fancy of the scribes, who penned letters in vain for the washerwomen, who clapped in time for the itinerant musicians, who could play songs remembered only by the astrologer, who promised every trader, for better or worse, a safe return to this city of noise from the quiet of the desert. In the teahouse, misty shapes still told their tales. But every so often, the gnarled tea drinkers looked at the young, the smooth-faced looked at the old, and all wondered if somehow the world was passing them by.

On the fifth day before the khan's army razed the city, the supply of raisins in the market dried up so suddenly that the fruit seller could only shrug away his queue of customers. By midmorning there were no more dates. The street of the weavers soon shook with indignation. We are running out of silk—where is the week's shipment? the long hands, plucked from their looms, curved to ask. In the adjacent neighborhood, the scribes sent their pupils to the gates to see whether the illiterate guards were keeping the incoming ink to themselves, while in his mildewed tower, the astrologer brooded over turtle shells and began to suspect that only bad things could come from lines so thin. A restless muttering filled the schools. Crows flapped irritably about the rooftops. And women and men were still making love, except for the captain of the guard, whose regular tryst with his squat girl was delayed by a mob of bent tailors and watery-eyed scribes' apprentices.

No, his guards hadn't taken their supplies, he said, and no, he didn't know why the caravans hadn't arrived. Would the kind citizens please not crowd before the gate? And would they return to their quarters and not disturb the city with their tantrums? It was left to the younger guards to disperse the mob and, later, as the day passed into the heat, to receive the breathless rider and his foaming horse and the bad news that always comes on the backs of such creatures. The caravans will not come today, nor tomorrow, nor for all eternity perhaps. The routes are blocked by an army the size of which I've never seen—it approaches the city. The guards peered toward the horizon and for once saw not the heat rippling from the bleached earth, nor the returning black humps of traders, but a faint smudge of dust.

The people were informed: our city is in grave peril, an army marches on us. An envoy was sent galloping into the distance. Jostling along the walls and atop the towers, the people squinted after him and wondered, How strange it is to fear a tuft of dust. Proclamations were issued urging calm and unity in the face of the enemy and nailed to the doors of shops, and banners were raised in the markets and squares that called for strength and patience and denounced the spread of rumors as a threat to the city. Everyone took the signs seriously and agreed, for writing is true knowledge revealed. But the denizens of the teahouse still told their tales. They too understood that truth lives only in the word and never in a single, bitter syllable of their breath.

Four days before the khan's army razed the city, the teahouse opened early and speculation began with the calls of the morning crows. The tea drinkers drained their cups in questions: Do they come to pillage and leave? Or do they come to conquer and stay? Should we negotiate? Is there no reasoning with them? Can we even talk to them, or will our words fall on their barbarian ears like rain on the senseless mountains?

And answers took shape in the steam. A tea drinker with a voice as round and rattling as a kettle stood up: They come to pillage, but they won't stay, because they'll leave nothing behind. We'd seal our fate if we tried negotiations. These barbarians think of diplomacy as a sure sign of weakness. In any case, they speak no tongue we could understand, instead favoring the language of birds and of the grunting creatures of the steppes. But you shouldn't think mountains are unfeeling, he said in a tinny rebuke; like old women, the mountains store aches in their bowels.

The teahouse tittered. As a fresh batch of tea steeped in the whistling samovar, questions percolated from the misty cups. In the land that they come from, do the men let their hair hang long and straight and tuck it into their belts? Do they stiffen it short with starch and lime? Do their caftans shine golden through the dust? Or do they ride over the land wild and bare-chested?

A sugary voice answered: They come from the cold, windy lands to the north, so their hair has to be thick and plentiful to keep them warm. It also makes a cushion for the many nights they sleep on the open plain. They are meticulous with their clothing, whatever it may be, especially on the warpath. All you men, even nomad men, are as vain as the next.

And the tea drinkers murmured. Nomads emerge every so often from the wilderness. They pour down on civilization, ravage cities, steal women and children, burn books, uproot the cabbages. But then what? They disappear into thin air, back into the unmapped earth, and nobody remembers them.

Not true. My grandmother still sings the old songs about Tukhluk Beh. He came from the roof of the world, smashing city after city after city, until one day, when there was nothing left to smash, he decided it was time to rebuild everything again. She says the spirits of his soldiers live on in today's builders and stonemasons.

Have you heard the tale, someone else asked, of Timur the Studious? He brought his army down from the mountains to attack monasteries and temples. Surrounded by gold, jewels, and silks, his men were only allowed to steal the written word.

Timur then built the largest library in the world, but even till his death, he never knew how to read.

What about Obruk Han? Spurned by the woman he cherished most, he left his disconsolate steppes for a life of war. He plotted his path of devastation from city to city deliberately so that the gods in the heavens could see his devotion to this woman. Obruk had written her name across the earth. From those letters of ash, we get our word for love.

I don't know these stories of yours, rattled the kettle voice. But let me tell you this: we'd best start praying to all the gods we can muster, especially the gods of the nomads. The city guards are dull and fat as old dogs. We'll have to get the gods on our side.

The sugary voice slipped in. Suppose this army keeps no gods and follows only the rhythm of their horses over the prairie? The question dropped into a tide of silence. The answer was clear. In that case, the tea drinkers had to agree, we are surely doomed.

Three days before the khan's army razed the city, the teahouse owner brought out pastries and water pipes, leavening conversation with the smell of jasmine and a thick purple smoke that made it difficult to roll one's *r*'s. The teahouse patrons watched the steam rise from their cups, while one drinker, between bites that shook her jowls, wondered about food. How often do they eat? Did they pack their flatbread in sacks of jute or linen? Did they cook with cloves or cinnamon? Would they spare our bakeries and bakers if they knew the taste of honey pastries, pistachio and almond, yogurt cooked through with winter sap from the forests?

The answers came in swift succession. They eat as often as we do—when the sun is rising, when the sun has ceased to rise, when the sun is setting, and when the stars reign in the night. Only they do not keep the prescribed fast days and, indeed, choose those days to eat in excess.

They keep their flatbread in bags of linen. It must be impossible for them—who come from the west—to get jute, since, as it is, the stuff arrives at great price and in small quantity in our markets from the faraway east, from a land of thick jungles and rivers where, in the summer, water floats from the earth to meet the clouds.

They cook with neither cinnamon nor cloves, since they are men of blood, not commerce, and find such tastes disagreeable.

They will spare our bakeries, since even barbarians understand the sanctity of the oven. But they will kill the bakers, who are all men of craft and discipline, the very opposite of the nomad. So when our city is reduced to ash and rubble, and the crows are pecking out our eyes, and our young boys and girls have been dragged to their unholy tents, they will warm themselves in the glow of the ovens and eat the very last crumbs of our famous cakes.

But if they spare the bakeries for the oven, some asked, why not the potteries for the red kiln? Or the smithies for the hearth and wheezing bellows? Or, for that matter, this teahouse for its whistling samovar?

They won't bother looting this place, said the kettle-voiced man. What could they want from here? Not our wealth, for we have none. Not our beauty, since clearly even you, my dear, he said, nodding in the direction of the jowls, have seen better days. And not our wisdom, for that, we know, has never been our vocation. The kettle-voiced man let his hands fall to his thighs in a soft slap, as if to emphasize the last point with the sound of a full stop.

The jowls quivered, biting into another pastry. And a buttery-voiced teenager, who preferred the dark soliloquies of the teahouse to scuffles on rooftops or the winks and pinches of the market, spoke. What would happen if the army came and destroyed everything but left this place standing? Would we just sit here like before and drink our tea with ruin all about us?

Most of us would, someone said, but you won't—people like them hack their way across the world to find tender little things like you. You'd best start stretching, another said dryly, it'll make the next few weeks less painful. And the buttery voice broke into a series of clotted sobs. The teahouse rebounded with hisses and reprimands. There was no point to honesty in a time of cold truths.

A voice as smooth as milk swallowed the din. We sow the seeds of our destruction by speaking of it. Let us retreat to the enemy, return to their food. She willed among the tea drinkers a fresh mood of imagination. They know only flesh, one said, hot and red off the bone. They let their cattle roam unwatched, confident that nobody will dare steal from them. They have forked tongues, another said, and when they gather to feast, their tongues snake in and out in wet harmony.

They eat peacock roasted with cashews for virility and drink whale oil for long life. But they get drunk on lizard blood fermented in the horns of the antelope. They cook animals whole with all the organs in place, eating the eyes first, since those are any creature's most powerful parts, and chucking the ears, since they believe the world of sounds is an illusion. Their appetites greatly outstrip ours because in truth they each have two stomachs to fill and two belly buttons to clean every night. In the worlds of men and beasts, nothing is produced that they have not at some point considered consuming.

How many animals must their army butcher for each meal?

Approximately two thousand, the kettle answered. Behind

the soldiers, the creaking engines of war, the dancers, chefs, and blacksmiths, there trail twelve legions of sheep. They have at their disposal a further ten companies of bulls, lowing through the dust, six flights of chickens, a scraggly militia of goats, and one platoon of ostriches.

Who, then, tends to the animals?

The kettle wasted no time in explaining. In formation alongside the animals march squadrons of shepherds and farmhands, milkmaids, gamesmen, and, of course, butchers with shears and cleavers. And before the meticulous logic of the teahouse could ask, What, then, do these attendants eat? the kettle continued: There follows in turn a caravan of wagons loaded with grain and bread to feed them and a detachment of hoary tailors to clothe them and a gang of blacksmiths to sharpen their blades. At the very end of the line, the army keeps the storytellers, who, though expected to warm the nightly fires with quaint tales, spend most of their time gossiping and lying to each other.

The tea drinkers allowed themselves a ripple of laughter, which slipped beyond the walls of the little shack into the sighs of the evening. Elsewhere in the city, children peeked into their mothers' kitchens to see what was for dinner. It was aubergine. In the courts, a judge rushed his sentencing of a man guilty of bribery, because even magistrates grow tired of being looked at. A vegetable seller emptied her unsold artichokes into the gutters. The moneylenders packed up their abacuses in clittering clats. And the tanners, knee-deep in pigeon excrement and blood, washed the leathery smell of death from their feet. Bitterly, they slunk away. Amid this folding of day into night, the laughter of the teahouse came as a whisper of that impossible life without creases.

Men and women returning home on their dusk-lit way hissed at the sight of the clay shack glimmering in the lamplight, with its wooden latch door open and its chattering patrons reclined within. Beggars spat against its walls, while the crows now chose its tiled roof for their nightly covenant. Imperceptible from within the teahouse, the city was turning against it. And imperceptible it would have remained for the tea drinkers (nestled on benches, nibbling pastries, tasting visions in tongues of smoke) had a passing porter (back breaking, body caked with dust and sweat) not thrust his head through the window. "This is a time for jokes?" he snarled. "We are about to be destroyed and all you do is make fun of us." The teahouse grew silent. Its shuttered lamps winked out, and slowly the drinkers padded home.

Two days before the khan's army razed the city, the tea drinkers invited a shadow puppeteer to preside over the day's discussions. While the small stage was built in the darkest corner, the woman with quivering jowls delivered a sermon on the necessity of vocation.

When men came together at the very first, all was rather primitive. We lived like the nomads, devoting our lives to the process of accumulating food. After time, of course, we began to grow plants and grain, and harvest the meat of cattle, and settle in towns. We became architects, builders, farmers, traders, smiths, warriors, and priests. In all this, it can be said that the crafts distinguish the later phase from the earlier—we are city dwellers and not nomads, for we have in our ranks people who can be described as tailors and cooks, while the nomads do not. But the question can be asked: Don't the nomads have crafts of their own? Are there not some who raid villages, some who tend the fires, some who make the bows and fletch the arrows, some who draw milk from the mares, some who beat filigree from gold, some who stitch their leather clothes, some who tell stories, some who whisper prophecies? The real difference between the nomad and us has little to do with these men of action; it is precisely because a city like ours has a teahouse, and keeps men of inaction—who produce nothing, whose only responsibility is to the leisure of thought—that the society of the city is different from that of the wild. And so, I submit to you, my colleagues, that we have no reason to feel shame for our work. It is we who give this city meaning.

The kettle-voiced man shook his wizened head, and parted his toothless gums to let forth the warm sounds of tin. My sister, unfortunately there are others in the city who produce nothing. Think of the philosophers, sitting in their windowless libraries. Or the astrologers watching the stars from their towers. Or the historians growing old in the archives. The teahouse and we are only a few among many beings of inaction.

No, not at all, insisted the milky voice. The philosophers instruct the teachers, who in turn instruct the children. For bits of coin, the astrologers come down from their towers and ply the people with omens. In their tomes, the historians record the lives of the city, the riots and celebrations, the great heroes and villains, the events both pedestrian and extraordinary that make up our days. She sipped tea to clear the gravel from her throat. And us? The city has no need for us, and we have no need for the city.

And some tea drinkers rushed to the obvious refutations: Where is it that you think you sleep, then? Where were you born? From whom do you buy your clothes and fine jewelry? But the woman with the quivering jowls smiled, saying that yes, that was exactly what she had meant all along, we have no necessary function and yet we still belong. Wasn't that the miracle of the city?

As she spoke, elsewhere in the city a pair of twins plotted

mischief in the park, a child spied on her parents fighting in the kitchen, students rose from their recitations and wondered to what use they would put all these words, and a sentry stood atop the wall, framed against the thickening cloud of dust. Hands folded against his chest, he prayed for the miracle that would save the city.

On offer in the teahouse was the miracle of birth. A shuttered lantern beamed onto the canvas screen raised in the corner. Standing dimly to the side, the puppeteer dipped his hands into the flickering river of light. Shadows began to plod about the canvas. At first, the tea drinkers struggled to make sense of the black shapes, mute nothings for minds aged in sound. But recognition dawned from the dark. The shadows swirled and writhed, and as the puppeteer introduced props—paper cutout puppets, gossamer rivers, tissue clouds, bead-glass skirts, a chain of paper birds—the teahouse found itself in the midst of a story known to all that needed no words: the tale of the founding of the city.

Once upon a time, there were two sisters who had fled from a faraway land to find a new place to live. The first was tall and foolish, and the second was short and wise. They searched and searched through deserts and over mountain peaks until at last they came to a lush green valley. Clear streams trickled down from the mountains, watering rich orchards of apple and pear. Flowers carpeted the valley floor. The first sister jumped for joy. "Here we can stay forever, safe and happy!" she cried. But the second sister was less sure. Some nagging suspicion gnawed at her (the puppeteer made tiny gauze flies buzz inside her stomach). *While the first sister set about building her house, the second went for a walk to calm her nerves.*

Elsewhere in the city, atop the parapets, the guards whiled away the dwindling hours playing dice. The dust cloud grew lazily throughout the day, but soon, out of the haze, a black speck appeared, quickly coming across the empty expanse in between. A rider approached the walls. The city's envoy had returned.

She came up to one of the peaks that flanked the valley, and there she found a hawk. "Little sister," the hawk said, "do not stay in this valley. Its charms deceive." And the second sister was not surprised, for she always knew that her instincts were right. "How do they deceive, Hawk?" she asked. "Simply," the hawk explained. "In winter the mountain passes will freeze shut, the streams will harden, the trees will grow heavy with ice, and you will be trapped. The vultures will descend upon you and leave no trace behind (the puppeteer sent a flight of long-beaked shadows to peck at the girl's eyes). *You both must leave."*

The envoy no longer had his eyes, nose, or ears. They had left only his mouth in place. He rocked gently on the back of his horse in the town's open square, where the people of the city gathered, anxious for news. "First they took my eyes, but before losing sight, I saw a flash of iron—armored soldiers in the thousands. Then they took my ears, but before I lost them, I heard the grinding of their bootsteps, like pounding in a mill. Last they took my nose, but I smell even now the smoke and ash in their wake." He shook his cratered head. "We cannot resist them. Many cities lie behind them, broken, torn to the ground, their peoples enslaved. We must flee."

"But, Hawk, where can we go? We have looked everywhere and found no place suitable," the second sister said. "Go north into the plains. After many days walking you will find a nomad's horse being eaten by vultures. Chase the vultures away, bury the horse, and make your home there." The wise sister thanked the hawk and went to fetch the first sister, but she would not be moved. "We've walked and walked, then we finally come to a beautiful, safe place, and now you want to leave? No, go where you please, but I'm staying." The second sister pleaded and wept, but there was no moving the elder. Her eyes brimming

with tears (the puppeteer dribbled wax down the doll's cheeks), *she left her sister, promising to return once she had found the spot described by the hawk.*

The envoy slumped from his horse and was carried away on a litter. A dense quiet settled in the square. No one spoke. In some nearby street, a woman leaned out a window to beat the dust from her oblivious quilts. Stray cats scratched and shrieked over a bowl of milk, while in his clay tower, an astrologer snored in the afternoon heat. He slept through the tumult at his very doorstep, as the crowd finally broke into a gray gust of talk:

What can we do?

Where can we go?

There's nowhere to go, they'll catch us wherever we run.

Armies have come before and been defeated.

Yes, this city's been here forever, it can survive any enemy.

In that case, you won't need me, I'm off.

What?

Me too.

You'd rather be speared in the wild than safe behind these walls?

We'll take our chances.

Such treachery. You're more useless than the tea drinkers.

At least we know what's happening outside the walls.

Go outside then, but whoever runs, know that we'll never let you back in.

So be it.

On pain of death.

The home of my soul is my body, not my city. My home is my own, not the one that would reject me.

God willing you'll be alive to be turned away.

God willing you'll be alive to be so stern.

She descended from the mountain passes until after many lonely days through hills and forests she came into the grasslands (the puppeteer had suitable cutouts for each terrain). *Then she went north, traveling only when the sun was up, so as not to lose her way. After some time, she found the nomad's horse that was being eaten by vultures, chased the vultures away with shouts and kicks* (the puppeteer had stitched ingenious joints on the paper legs), *and with great effort buried the horse. She then surveyed the land. There was a slow brown river nearby, low hills in the distance, and a forest not too far away. The soil was thin, but still soft and wet. But most important, she decided, the place was not hemmed in, and that, she knew, was the great advantage of her future home: it was open to the world.*

News chased rumor through the city, and soon the streets filled with the scrambling of refugees heading into exile. By dusk, the gates were sealed shut, and the sobbing of those beyond disappeared into that exhausted background drone of the countryside. The exiles' hope: to be forgotten is to become invisible, but to become invisible is not to be forgot.

Those who remained were nervous, but worse, they were idle. With nothing to sell, the fruit sellers gathered in prickly clumps, sharing the last of the grapes and spitting seeds into the gutters. The scribes decided to test their apprentices' handwriting, so the watery youths yet again drained their eyes on forgotten legal codes and historical almanacs. The weavers looked resentfully at each other's looms and wondered why another's looked so much newer. The butchers wrinkled their noses at the smell of flesh. The cobblers paced barefoot. The porters slumped their shoulders of stone. The guards carved their names into the walls. The carpenters didn't see the point in making coffins, while the manuscript illuminators took no pride in the color red. The ring of hammer on anvil sounded hollow to the blacksmiths, and in his dusty tower the astrologer woke from his dreams feeling vengeful—everywhere, he tasted blood.

It began, as most things end, with dogs. Tussling outside the teahouse, a gang of strays caught sight of the lurching shadows within and decided—with irrefutable canine logic—to bark. Passersby looked in. A curious handful soon cocooned into an indignant crowd. In times of stress, people like to exercise their lowest faculties. They whispered:

They're playing games.

Always the same, no respect.

No time for triviality, this.

(And the tone hardened as word spread.)

They're making fun of us.

Always the same, do-nothings.

I break my back every day for this city while they sit about drinking tea.

(And the tone darkened as the people of the city shook their fists.)

How can we allow this indolence in our city?

We're being punished, punished for their decadence.

It's they who make us vulnerable, they who make us weak.

(And the people of the city found strength in their fear.)

We'd be better off without them.

Bring it down.

Tear it down.

Burn, burn, burn, burn.

From the inside of the teahouse, the crescendo of the street seemed only to echo the drama of the shadows. *In her chosen home, the second sister built a strong house made of clay, wood, and straw. And before it she raised stone gates to keep herself safe, but would allow other lonely travelers inside. After some time, and with her new home secure, she decided to return to the mountains and fetch the first sister from the green valley. She journeyed long and hard and soon she reached the high mountains. The wind bit at her ankles* (the puppeteer depicted "wind" with streams of silk ribbons), *and the frost crunched beneath her feet. And when she had climbed to the entrance of the valley, she could find no way in. The passes were thick with snow; a blizzard shook the ceiling of the world.* (Hands thrust through the windows, feet knocked down the door.) *She sank down in despair and wept. Seeing her, the hawk whirled down from his mountain perch.* (Tables were flung aside, cups smashed, a fiery brand skittered across the floor.) *"I told you, little sister, to leave the valley, for its charms deceive. Why have you come back?" The wise sister sobbed. "Oh, Hawk, my sister stayed and now I've come to bring her back with me. But I can't find a way inside." And the hawk shook his head. "You are too late. It is winter, the season of the vultures."* (The puppeteer cast away his puppets, and against the rising flame, the mob's shadows swarmed across the screen.)

The hawk flew away and brought back all that was left of the impatient sister: the ears. Then, the wise sister went away to her home, and she buried her sister's remains with due ceremony. On her sister's tomb—which now lies beneath the city—she chiseled a solemn epitaph. LISTEN TO YOUR HEART, FOR THE EYES DECEIVE. *What she really meant to write was: "In every creation, there is always loss."*

The day before the khan's army razed the city, pupils sat down for their geography lessons. "Where the sun rises," they recited, "and the world begins, there lies the land of Qin. To the south, at the foot of the earth, is al-Hind, protected by mountains and watered by the oldest of rivers. In the north, forests stretch empty to a sea of churning ice. The sun sets over Europe and Maghreb to the west."

And around us, the teacher asked, which countries do we live among?

"Khorasan, Fars, Gandhara, Bactria, Sogdiana, Mesopotamia."

And the cities?

"Balkh, Herat, Samarqand, Merv, Zeugma, Otrar, Ai-Khanoum."

Rivers?

"Amu Darya, Syr Darya, Hari Rud, Aras."

Mountains?

"Damavend, Sabalan, Elbrus, Ararat, Bam-i-dunya, and the Muztag."

The teacher didn't ask about the peoples in their midst, the tribes beyond their walls. Geography is never flesh but stone, water, and clay, names and lines and vacant scratches of the plume. And the students, skeptics to the end, wondered: How could clouds of dust rise from a world engraved in flat relief? Outside the school, soldiers rustled toward the city walls, where they relieved their comrades and took over the chore of playing dice on the parapets. The game lacked conviction. Few soldiers had the stomach for reckless wagers or the hunger for their fellows' rings. Embarrassed, a man returned a belt he had won off another. This was no time for gain. Dust hung high on the horizon, and beneath it, invisible to the eye, a river of flesh rolled on to flood the city.

Even as the khan's army neared, the city continued to drift. In the baths, slaves untangled their mistresses' hair with ivory combs. A baker left his cakes to cool in the shade. Wardens patrolled the market for pickpockets, though few stalls remained open and fewer shoppers roamed the quiet lanes, mistrusting the onions. Only the booksellers were out in force, possessed of that blind faith in text. There will always be books to sell. There will always be people to read.

In the gutted teahouse, the tea drinkers gathered at dusk,

looking at each other wordlessly, their faces open books. Smoke still lifted off the wreckage, drifting over the streets, a thin echo of the horizon of dust closing on the city. They could not bring themselves to speak. Neighborhoods of rust had overtaken the voice of the kettle, the sugar had grown hard in the heat, the milk gone sour, the jowls cobwebbed and creased. Above the smoldering ruins, the city hummed its commentary. And the tea drinkers knew: The past is read in the sands, not heard. In later years, archaeologists would find no trace of the teahouse or its strata of myth. But the drinkers remained there, silent and unmoving, until the untold ends of their stories.

ELEPHANT AT SEA

In the late summer of 1979, the Second Secretary of the Indian embassy to Morocco received a cable that uprooted his considerable years of training and left him floundering. The message read simply: "Elephant en route." Was it some sort of code? Further investigation only deepened his confusion. The cable had come from the customs office in Cochin, a port in the south of India. No, the customs officials reported back to him, it wasn't code. It was an elephant, an elephant that along with its mahout—its driver—was now very much headed by ship to Casablanca. The Second Secretary probed: Why send an elephant? Here at the customs office, the reply came, we handle only the movement of goods. For the movement of reasons, please refer your inquiry to the ministry of external affairs.

The Second Secretary telegrammed his colleagues in the ministry in Delhi. With telegrams to the ministry, it was important, first, to be terse so that you were considered economical and, second, to be sharp so that in the midst of reams of communication from outposts around the world, your message would be noticed. WHY SHIP ELEPHANT STOP EMBASSY ALREADY HAS CARS STOP. No one in the ministry seemed to know anything about the elephant. A flummoxed telegram returned to the embassy. WHAT ELEPHANT STOP IS THIS CODE STOP. Embarrassed, the Second Secretary finally consulted the ambassador, who knew through long experience that it was pointless to question the whims of the capital. Marvelous, the ambassador said, smoothing his mustache, an elephant, just what we need, and they couldn't even send it to us . . . no, they're sending it to Casablanca. You'll have to arrange for the thing to be met and picked up. He sprayed himself with cologne and mused: If an elephant can even be picked up.

That night the Second Secretary swam awake in his bed, resenting the sheets, resenting the pillow, resenting the indifference of his work, resenting Morocco, resenting Arabic for its impossible, secret throatiness, and resenting, with what little bitterness was left to him, the unknown buffoon who would make diplomacy out of elephants.

The buffoon was not, as he imagined, some self-satisfied civil servant in South Bloc, but the princess of Morocco. Explanation arrived via telex from a friend in the ministry who owed him a few favors and so mustered the initiative to ask around. The story of the elephant began six years earlier in the same Indian embassy in Rabat. At one of those habitual functions whose purpose seems so obvious in the preparation but disappears in the operation, the little Moroccan princess had come to the embassy and frozen before a picture of an elephant. It was among the many stock images—all approved by the ministry of tourism—that lined the lobby of the embassy: dawn over the Himalayan ranges; houseboats on the backwaters; the Taj Mahal rosy in its cushion of smog; a bright tractor devastating a field of wheat. The princess only had eyes for the elephant. Her wordless arm extended toward the picture, pointing. *C'est un éléphant*, said the embassy official tasked with escorting the princess. She remained transfixed. *Vous aimez les éléphants?* the unlucky man suggested. It seemed the princess did love elephants, because she wouldn't move. The official, who had in previous posts offered counsel on trade policy with Indonesia and arms deals with the Soviet Union, looked around for help before lowering himself to her level. *Mademoiselle, vous voulez un éléphant?* he asked with the desperation stoked in him by all children—never mind the princess of Morocco. She turned, smiled, and gave him the smallest gift of a nod. It was enough. The official eventually spoke to the then ambassador, who put in the request to Delhi recommending the delivery of an elephant to satisfy the princess and to strengthen a bilateral friendship. The request passed through the appropriate channels at the usual speeds. Six years later, the creature was irrevocably on its way.

The Second Secretary received updates about the elephant's progress from various consular staff. In Aden, it posed for photographs in front of the oldest coffeehouse. It bumped a football back and forth with boys on the beach in Alexandria. In Algiers, veterans of the war against the French held a reception in its honor; the Indian elephant was, in their words, a symbol of the ancient wisdom of a civilization that had inspired the global struggle against Western imperialism. After it passed through Gibraltar, the Second Secretary got an excited telegram from the British naval high command. BRILLIANT STOP TOP PACHYDERM STOP.

The Moroccans were less enthused. What are we to do with it? they said. Casablanca's zoo has enough African elephants, and there's no space for an Indian one. The Second Secretary protested. It's for the princess, he reminded them, she asked for it. Well, she may have, the Moroccans said, but she's away studying sociology in Paris now and has no interest in elephants. So you might have to take the thing back.

Only the Indian ambassador's persistence at a cocktail party won their grudging cooperation. It was agreed that the elephant would be specially housed in a portion of the royal gardens in

Rabat. How it would get there was another matter. The Moroccans insisted they had no trucks big enough to carry the creature between the two cities. This was a time of war and their heaviest military vehicles were all rumbling around the south. Worse, thanks to the mischief of Polisario terrorists, the single rail line between Casablanca and the capital was broken. But these inconveniences, the Moroccans claimed, shouldn't be a problem. After all, the elephant is its own means of transportation.

The Second Secretary was sent to Casablanca to escort the elephant back to Rabat. It took some time to find an appropriate launch in which to ferry the creature to port. When it finally disembarked, the small police band awaiting its arrival had grown sour in the heat. They rushed the welcoming ditty and swiftly packed away their trombones. The reporters also sped through their work. They found the mahout altogether too clothed. As he perched on the elephant's back, they had him remove his shirt and roll up his trousers to look more convincing for the cameras, all knobby knees and gleaming skin. Instead of asking the mahout questions about the elephant, they surrounded the Second Secretary—he was wearing a suit. We are proud to share the joy of elephants with the people of Morocco, he said. The *haathi* belongs not to one nation, but to all.

What little the Second Secretary knew about elephants came from an urban childhood of zoos and encyclopedias. As a measure of their robust memories, elephants hold grudges and harbor very finely developed notions of revenge. Elephants have sensitive feet capable of feeling through the earth, from long distances away, the approach of other elephants, or of rainstorms, or of bulldozers. Studies have shown that they can recognize their own reflections, suggesting that, however rudimentary, there may exist among elephants an amorphous theory of mind.

In sum, these scraps formed an altogether surreal idea of the elephant, one incommensurate with the full being in front of him, dappled with cooling splashes of mud, blinking restlessly and curling its trunk around the legs of its driver. The mahout supplied more practical information. In its present, ship-weary condition, the elephant could walk at most forty kilometers in a single stretch, probably no more than twenty-five. How far is it to the capital? he asked. He spoke no Hindi, and the Second Secretary spoke no Malayalam, so they talked in a manner of English. A little more than ninety kilometers to Rabat, the Second Secretary said. Hoisting himself onto the elephant, the mahout surveyed the road leading out from the docks through the flat outskirts of Casablanca. For all the immensity of this unknown continent, the world always seemed more manageable from the back of an elephant. He smiled at the Second Secretary. Ninety of their Moroccan kilometers or ninety of ours? What are you talking about, the Second Secretary said, there's no difference. The mahout shook his head. You and I may not be able to tell the difference, but the elephant can.

In consultation with the two Moroccan gendarmes assigned to them, they agreed to break journey several times en route to Rabat. The convoy set out from Casablanca in the middle of the afternoon. The gendarmes led in their battered white car, its red lettering chipped and peeling. The Second Secretary brought up the rear in the embassy's sedan. In the middle, the mahout set a gentle tempo. The elephant wore an anklet that, wrapped around a man, would have had all the thickness of chains. Its every step tinkled with the jewelry of another land.

Perhaps because it was on its way to await the uncertain pleasure of a princess, or perhaps because it had already traveled so far, the elephant chose not to exert itself. But it quickened its pace whenever the coastal road veered west toward the Atlantic.

The change would have been imperceptible to observers—and there were many on the busy highway—but the mahout felt it in his thighs. Each time the cobalt ocean wheeled into view, the creature's muscles seemed to quiver with new desire. It was an urge all the more palpable in its restraint; elephants are polite creatures of typically conservative temperament. Yet it was enough of a rumble and churn for the mahout to sense that his mount was already missing the sea.

At dusk, the elephant drank from a pond in the golf course of Mohammedia, a pleasant-enough beach town that brushed up against Morocco's only oil refinery. The last of the day's players lofted their balls in long arcs overhead before descending on the fairway and finding the creature asleep in a bunker. It lay on its side flanked by the apologetic guards, its heavy breathing raising little tempests of sand. Nobody protested. Golf can only be improved by the intrusion of an elephant, even a snoring one.

The Second Secretary was given accommodation in the clubhouse, in a room glowing with trophies and the lidless glare of the nearby refinery. He smoked and dipped at a plate of *zaalouk*. The mahout came in but declined the invitation to share in the dish. He had already eaten with the policemen. The Second Secretary gestured to a couch for the mahout to sleep on. The man looked restless. No, I'll stay with the elephant, he said, this is our first night back on land after weeks . . . It will rest poorly without me, and I without it. The Second Secretary shrugged and returned to his puréed eggplant, only to be surprised by the touch of the mahout's hand on his shoulder. In the parallel universe of their own country, such contact would be almost unimaginable, a movement far too intimate to cross the wide gulf of rank. Indians turn into more equal beings when not at home.

Tell me truthfully, the mahout leaned forward. There are no

other elephants in Rabat? The Second Secretary sighed. I've told you already, it will have to be kept by itself. The royal gardeners can only manage one elephant. It will have all its creature comforts, don't worry. The mahout listened, seesawing his head from side to side. This was the strongest and happiest elephant he had ever known, but he feared that it would struggle with its solitude. Like humans, elephants yearn for other elephants. It will be lonely, he said, it will need distractions. Annoyed, the Second Secretary promised they would make sure that it was the most distracted elephant in Africa. He unlaced his shoes and stretched out to sleep.

A few hours later, with the red and orange light of the refinery's towers angling upon his face, he awoke to find the mahout sitting cross-legged in front of him. I'm sorry to disturb you, the mahout said, but promise me something: you won't let them use it in the circus. In the circus? the Second Secretary said. The mahout climbed to his feet and paced about the room. In the circus, yes . . . I have heard about the way the *firangs* treat elephants—like dolls, like puppets, like cartoons. He grew more animated still. They make them dance, they make them ride cycles, they make them stand on their heads . . . sometimes, they think it is amusing to have the animals sit down to tea as if they were old women . . . this can't be its fate. The Second Secretary sat up. We won't let that happen, he said, besides, you have nothing to worry about; these people aren't really *firangs*, they're Moroccans, they're so much like us . . . Just go to sleep.

But mahouts sleep as fitfully as elephants, and when the Second Secretary rose at dawn to perform his ablutions, he found the man at the door of the clubhouse, standing in a pose of total stillness at war with the anxious writhing of his eyebrows. The mahout burst at the sight of the secretary. These royal gardens, are they near the water? The water? the Second Secretary said, blinking. Yes, the water—the ocean. I have no idea, the Second Secretary replied. The mahout held the Second Secretary's hand in both of his. The elephant . . . for it to be happy, it must be near the sea.

As he shaved, the Second Secretary muttered to himself about the mahout. All the man has to do is deliver the elephant to Rabat, and then the government will give him a tidy check and send him home by plane. How many mahouts ever see the inside of a plane? He'll never again get to be in a plane. He can tell his parents, his wife, his children if he has any, his grandchildren in the future, that he was in a plane. And they'll tell all their friends and enemies and the mahout will be forever famous throughout his village. Yet this madman keeps me awake all night with his ridiculous demands for an elephant nobody actually wants. If he fusses any more, we'll return him by boat. And what glory is there in a boat?

What the Second Secretary did not know—and what the mahout found impossible to explain—was that, for the elephant at least, travel by boat was utterly glorious. Before they left India, the mahout had worried about the creature's well-being. How would it cope in steerage for all those weeks? Would it endure the din of the ship's innards, the engines and pipes pumping at all times, soot-faced engineers swinging like monkeys from the levers? Surely, the clamor of a mechanical universe would depress a creature that loved nothing more at the end of the day than lowering itself into mud. The only consolation the mahout could find was that he too was terrified of the ship. There was solidarity to be had between two beings who had never traveled further than Kozhikode, two beings for whom the rusting expanse of an oceangoing ship was only ever something to behold, not enter. In its salty dark, the mahout imagined, they would comfort each other, leaning close, pressing head to trunk.

It was not to be. While the mahout lurched from deck to deck vomiting, the elephant thrilled to life at sea. It trumpeted every time the captain sounded the great foghorn. The ship's sailors fawned over the creature, playing it music, showering it with nuts and chocolate. There were pleasures to be had even in its hold in the cargo bay, which rattled with the vigor of the ship's machinery. One morning, the mahout discovered the elephant rumbling. With its usual smile, it produced a low and eerie noise that seemed to come from its most interior parts. The mahout rushed to its side and held it as best as he could, trying to calm the animal. A moment's listening dispelled his fears; in perfect pitch, the elephant was mimicking the sound of the engines, as if through imitation it could bridge the divide between thought and matter and speak with the gray monstrosity of the ship.

On deck, the elephant stormed from side to side, relishing the heave of the ship, the rise and prostration of the bow as it carved its mass through the blue. The mahout studied the joy of the elephant with awe. He thought the elephant would grow bored of the sea, but the wonder never wore off. As the wind sprayed it with foam, the creature seemed to admire the uninterrupted ocean in a kind of rapture, a dervish-like ecstasy. It once occurred to the mahout that this was the closest he had ever got to witnessing contact with the divine: the elephant forgetting its elephantness in the vista of the sea, the veils of *moksha* parted, the creature poking its trunk into the beyond and feeling its way toward cosmic oneness. Then the motion of the vessel shook the mahout's insides loose. He staggered to the rim of the stern and emptied himself into the deep.

The sailors also felt the magic of the elephant's presence. Once during the voyage, in the Indian Ocean, a solitary whale bobbed into view. This was hardly an unusual sight for the tanker's crew, but they watched anyway as the whale crested the surface and snorted through its blowhole. They hoped at that moment for a response from the elephant: a trumpet, a bellow, a spout of water from its trunk, some little signal of recognition. After all, what was a whale but an elephant of the sea? These two creatures were kin in bulk and grace, breathing the most air through the largest lungs in a world rightfully made for them. There could be no better omen than that shared understanding. For men who commit their bodies to the seas, who abandon childhoods on rice paddies and factory floors for the education of currents and gales on the shipways, the communion of these beasts would be vindication. But the sailors were disappointed. Standing on the opposite, starboard side, the elephant had not seen the whale at all. Or if it had, it chose to ignore it, keeping its eyes fixed instead in contemplation of the water.

On the golf course, the mahout found the elephant by the pond, its trunk lingering at its feet. He massaged the hard knot of muscle on its lower back, the corbeled arch that lifted the creature's mass from the earth. As he readied the elephant for the march on, he wondered how a journey across the seas could change someone. When the elephant regarded its reflection in the still water, did it see a being transformed? Could it? Maybe it was presumptuous of the mahout to think so grandly of the elephant's capacities, its self-awareness, its very sense of the possibility of a self. Perhaps this sad-eyed creature merely looked at the pond and thought: What a miserable excuse for a sea.

The convoy reached Skhirat in the early evening. On the way, the mahout had suggested to Adil, one of the Moroccan gendarmes (he had learned their names), that he come sit on the back of the elephant. Adil stripped off his uniform jacket, approached the elephant from the front, hesitated, crept around the side and kept creeping till he made a full circle, and looked imploringly up at the mahout. The mahout laughed. He scratched the back of the elephant's head and pressed one knee against its neck. It dipped to the ground. Adil tried to look the creature in the eye for reassurance, but it stared beyond him up the road, its ears flapping like fans. He grasped the mahout's forearm and heaved himself up, gripping the hairy hide with both hands as the elephant rose to its feet and lurched on.

Elephants respond to certainty, the mahout said. You do not need to charm them so much as direct them . . . Like us, they are logical creatures, and like us, they understand that the order of the universe dictates to them a certain place, a certain rank, a certain dependence on the demands of others. The mahout spoke in Malayalam, but Adil listened to the tumbling words anyway, trying his best to look ahead and not at the road swaying beneath him. The truth is, the mahout continued, that driving an elephant does not require intuition or special intelligence, only a willingness to command . . . more than that, a belief in your command.

Command was in his blood. The mahout was raised to ride elephants, as was his father, and his father's father, and as far as he knew all the males of their line snaking back to some letterless past, when man first wrestled the beast into obedience. No better life had presented itself to him than that of driving elephants. He was aware that many in his village were jealous of his trade, the princely work that saved him from the drudgery of the fields. When the news arrived that he would be sent with the elephant to Morocco, his family lit many candles to fend off the evil eye. You'll come back a big man, they said, and nobody wishes well for big men. He laughed them off: What nonsense!

I'll come back just the same . . . This isn't my journey, it's the journey of the elephant; I'm only an appendage of flesh. Adil squirmed behind him and cars passed, honking. I am commanded to command, the mahout thought, I am an instrument of command, I am an instrument.

From the trailing sedan, the Second Secretary watched the spectacle of the Moroccan gendarme clinging to the elephant. He was surprised to feel a degree of envy. No invitation to mount the elephant had been extended to him. If anyone should first get a turn on the elephant, he thought, it should be me, not that fellow. He filed this grievance away as yet more proof of the strangeness of the mahout and as further evidence, if he needed any more, of the unending injustice that was the daily life of a Second Secretary.

At Skhirat, Adil slid, nauseous, off the back of the elephant, attempted a few steps, and tumbled to his knees. The children of the village roared at his collapse and flocked about the elephant. Marouane, the other gendarme, dispersed them as best he could, but they remained bubbling in the corners of the village square, pantomiming the elephant and its minders. Skhirat's mayor, who was also its lead cleric, came to shake hands with the visitors and admire the creature. In normal circumstances, the village was used to strangers passing through; it was a stop on the Casablanca–Rabat rail line. But since the interruption of rail service, the place had grown dustier and quieter, and its people were happy to produce a welcome. They brought trellised tables into the square. Pitchers of fresh juices, cups of tea, and miraculous tagines came steaming from nearby houses. All the village's luminaries—its post office clerk, its librarian, its accountant, its letter-writer, its chief (and only) constable, its doctor, its farm veterinarian (who kept his distance from the elephant, eyeing the creature with trepidation), and so on—assembled to have a meal with the Second Secretary, who was made to repeat, over and over again, in slow French, the basic facts of his life and of his world. The children cheered as the elephant munched carrots dipped in *harissa*. The gathering continued till late in the evening. When the day's last *azaan* interrupted proceedings, the elephant raised its trunk toward the minaret and sounded back, bellowing in its own fashion the call to prayer. All the men of the village trundled away to the mosque except for the librarian, who patted the Second Secretary on the back and smuggled him home to share a bottle of arak.

During the night, the Second Secretary snored, drunk, on the librarian's sofa. Adil slept on a bench. The mahout tucked his chin into his knees and dozed against the slumbering bulk of the elephant. Marouane stood awake, vigilant for any mischievous children lurking at the edges of the square. Nothing happened until an hour before the morning *azaan*. A shape formed in the provincial gloom and drifted toward the elephant. It was the cleric-mayor. Peace be upon you, Marouane said. And you, the cleric-mayor returned. He rolled up the sleeves of his robe and worked his way around the horizontal elephant. I just want to check, he said half to himself, I just want to check. Marouane watched him dubiously. Check what? The cleric-mayor had already knelt by the elephant's loins. He startled. Well, I'm just curious if the creature is Muslim. In three strides, Marouane had grabbed him by the collar, dragged him away, and dropped him to the ground. He looked down on the older man. You fool, you bumpkin . . . Be decent and keep your crazy ideas to yourself . . . Does a donkey have religion? Can a donkey be Muslim? How can this animal be Muslim? The cleric-mayor straightened himself, jabbing a finger into Marouane's uniform. Boy, he snarled, have some respect . . . That peaceful creature is more of a man than any of your kind will ever be.

The commotion woke the elephant and by extension the mahout. Alarmed by the sudden rise of the animal, the cleric-mayor made apologetic noises and ghosted away. The mahout saw Marouane's agitation. He pointed at Adil sleeping on the bench, urging the gendarme to follow his colleague's example. Marouane nodded and slumped off. The elephant snorted. It stamped its feet. It wrapped its trunk around the mahout's waist, hugging the man close. Whatever beliefs it did possess, it certainly disliked being roused from its dreams.

The mahout stood for a little while, stroking the elephant's trunk until it sunk once more to its knees, then rolled to its side. They were alone in the village square. At this time before dawn in the mahout's own village, the roosters would be outdoing one another, the potholed roads would already be clanging with traffic, his family in their multitude would be scratching and groaning and clucking in the shared sleeping space. Morocco had so much room, so much silence. The mahout watched Skhirat take shape in the leavening dark. There was an enviable modesty to the even spread of low buildings, the humble bakery warming its ovens at the edge of the square, the grace of the mosque's silhouetted minaret, the peace of all its obscurity. He knew that this was a tiny country pinned between desert and sea. He knew that his own country was large by any estimation. And yet the calm of this small place felt infinite.

The elephant nuzzled his hand and murmured in its sleep. He buried his face in its ear. He whispered: Sleep well, my beauty, sleep well, my prince. If you dream, don't dream of home and don't dream of me. Dream of the sea. You and I are now so alone in this world . . . Dream of the sea, my life, dream of the sea.

The elephant seemed to sleep, but its trunk wrapped more tightly around the mahout. It refused to release him. As sensitive as the mahout was to each tremor of the elephant's body, so too was the creature attuned to its driver. It could feel the energy in the man, the insistent force pushing against bone and skin, so different from his usual ocean of calm. The mahout stroked the elephant's ear, the softer hairs of the inner flap and the harder exterior. After the elephant began to snore, the mahout leaned against the creature and wept. The elephant only shuddered in its sleep. Elephants, like humans, are capable of tears, but it's unclear if their tears have anything to do with emotions. As light began to escape down from the eastern mountains, the elephant loosened its grip and let the mahout go.

Dawn came with the first *azaan*. Adil shook awake, as did Marouane. The village crawled into its quiet, habitual motion, with the small aberration of an elephant sleeping at its center. The Second Secretary staggered to his sedan for his toiletries. By the time he finished brushing his teeth next to the well, both the gendarmes stood before him, delivering the news as best they could that the mahout had disappeared.

The Second Secretary was incredulous. Disappeared? Impossible. Skhirat was mobilized to find the mahout. Children swarmed the rooftops. Scooters buzzed down the road in both directions. Farmers turned over their cauliflowers. The chief constable furiously blew his whistle. There was no trace of the man. At the post office, the Second Secretary sent a message to the embassy. MAHOUT ABSCONDED STOP PLEASE ADVISE STOP. The Indian ambassador rang the post office. He's vanished, has he? The Second Secretary said he had. That's a real pity, the ambassador lamented, but what to do, it's pure physics . . . You propel an object a certain distance and you just can't expect it to come to rest, it will keep going forward. You take a man this far from his benighted village and he'll lose all interest in going back . . . so it goes. But, sir, the Second Secretary interjected, what do we do about the elephant? I don't know, the ambassador said, Rabat isn't all that far. Yes, the Second Secretary agreed, but how do we move the elephant? Why are you asking me? the ambassador snapped. If I were a mahout, I wouldn't be here having this bloody conversation with you, would I? Just do whatever it is you need to do.

The Second Secretary sat on the hood of his sedan, staring at the elephant. It looked back at him, long-lashed and indifferent. He imagined the various means at his disposal that would convince this accumulation of flesh to proceed down the last stretch of highway to the capital. Perhaps he could lay down a trail of carrots all the way to Rabat. Or maybe if all the children pushed hard enough, they could inch the elephant up the road. Or better yet, why not just leave the elephant here for the people of Skhirat? Why not be generous and gift them the problem?

Pitying the glum resignation of the Second Secretary, Adil was stirred to provide the solution himself. He came forward to the elephant and placed his hand behind its head, speaking to the creature in Arabic. It inspected Adil and blinked. Time to go, the gendarme said, and time to give me a lift. There was a pause, the kind of uncertain stillness that humans might call hesitation, but that elephants would of course understand differently. The creature bent down. Gingerly, Adil clambered on top. The elephant returned to its feet. Adil's prodding steered it onto the road. For the first time in two days, the Second Secretary smiled. *Allons-y!* he cried. *Allons-y!*

It was imperative to get going before Adil's luck ran out and the elephant decided to stop cooperating. The convoy reassembled and bid a hasty goodbye to Skhirat. All the villagers waved, except for the cleric-mayor. From the window of the mosque, he had seen the mahout slink away in the early hours, seen the alien gleam in his eyes, the rootless abandon of the wanderer. It was a sad spirit, one the cleric-mayor could not comprehend and dared not interfere with; who was he—who had never seriously left his village nor contemplated doing so—to judge the actions of a stranger come to a strange place? So he kept his peace. God be with you, the cleric-mayor said to the departing rump of the elephant, god be with you.

They had reached the outskirts of Rabat when the handlers from the royal gardens finally materialized and relieved them of the elephant. For the cameras, the ambassador posed in front of the creature with Adil, the hero who saved the day and strengthened the bonds between the people of India and Morocco. It was reported to the newspapers that the mahout had been incubating a mysterious tropical disease that killed him en route to Rabat. The ambassador asked the Second Secretary to ensure that Adil's wife received a very tasteful flower arrangement. The Second Secretary did as he was told.

When the princess returned during her holidays, she was enchanted by the elephant. She would lie next to it and read aloud her books of philosophy and critical theory. She introduced it to champagne. The princess was so enamored of the creature that she insisted it accompany her on a trip to the beach. The elephant hurried over the dunes at the sight of the ocean, the clarion call of its trunk greeting the waves. Everybody laughed as it played in the surf. It seemed to enjoy being knocked over in the shallows, finding its feet, retreating to the beach, and then wheeling its bulk around for another charge against the sea. It all seemed a pleasure, but the elephant was sad that no matter how earnestly it plunged into the water, the tide always drove it back to shore.

A UNITED NATIONS IN SPACE

In between sessions, the ambassadors come to the viewing vestibule and search the shadowed half of the earth. They crowd the portholes. Where once they might have seen the bright fuzz of cities and towns, now the dark patches are profound. It's not simply a case of the electricity being cut, the lights winking out, the streets and homes rolled away. No, Kiribati thinks, it's as if humanity's white webs have been colored black . . . a black more velvet than the night, continental in its spidery sprawl.

There are still pockets of lights here and there. Azerbaijan takes comfort in the glow nuzzling the Caspian. DRC beams at the sight of Kinshasa. A man of the pampas, Argentina crosses himself for good Rosario, sitting white on the shores of a new sea. If I'm honest, he thinks, I never cared much for Buenos Aires in the first place. A waiter enters with cups of coffee. Unapologetic, Panama helps herself to two.

Mexico sidles up to Luxembourg. That's his third, he says to her. Third what? Third glass of milk. They look at the Secretary-General, sleepless and slumped, milk limning his mustache, as he reaches up to shake the hand of the Holy See. Luxembourg shrugs. It's always morning in space, she says, and it's always bedtime in space. Mexico stares into his cup. At this rate, it won't be long before I have to take my coffee black.

The ambassadors troop into the council hall, a converted

lounge. A disco ball still hangs from the ceiling. The staff of the MaidenX Orbital Hotel consulted pictures of the original General Assembly and Security Council when arranging the chairs and tables, but they could manage only an approximation. The nameplates of each country bump against one another. There's little room for elbows, let alone for aides—staffers must follow proceedings elsewhere, listening to audio streams hunched in the main dining hall. When the council president calls the session to order, the ambassadors fumble for their earpieces.

For months amid its other work, the council has been trying to find a site where it might reinstall itself on earth. Bhutan's offer of his mountain capital was initially welcomed, largely because the Himalayas seemed the most secure place in a world scoured by the oceans. But then the noise of war spread up the valleys, big countries growled at each other over glaciers, and little Bhutan demurred, saying that this might not be the best time to discuss the logistics of diplomatic license plates. Australia put herself forward, evoking the immensity of the continent, but the island was too remote for many members; one may as well be in near-earth orbit as in the antipodes. The ambassadors debated the prospects of other sites, none proving palatable for the majority.

Now Botswana comes under consideration. She makes a modest case. The country's urban center remains more or less intact, not yet affected by the upheaval of the faraway coasts. The sorghum and millet crops have been strong this year. Gaborone could accommodate a version of the establishment that once held sway in midtown Manhattan, though of course there would not be the same range of amenities for delegates. Telecom speeds are among the fastest in Africa. From Gaborone, there are air links to many surviving cities, Nairobi, Bamako, Khartoum. I don't suppose there is a Turkish restaurant in Gaborone, Kazakhstan wonders aloud. Unfortunately not. Well, it's never too late to start one. Jordan says something and laughs, but the Arabic translator didn't make it on board the MaidenX, so nobody finds the joke particularly funny.

What about the price of diamonds? the Secretary-General asks, unintroduced. (In an early working-methods session, the council had agreed to loosen the structure of proceedings slightly, since all other structures in the world were loosened.) What about the price of diamonds? I understand it has skyrocketed. Yes, the world is finally recognizing the enduring value of Botswana's diamonds. Excellent, so were the Secretariat placed in Gaborone, it would require a share of the revenue from diamond exports. Botswana is shocked into silence. France and the United Kingdom nod sagely. As a sovereign country, Botswana says after a pause, Botswana retains full control of the tax revenue from trade across its borders. Borders, the Holy See snorts. Excuse me, Indonesia bristles at the Holy See, observers do not have the floor.

Belgium reaches down the table to touch Botswana on the arm. There is great prestige in hosting an international institution . . . this would only be a small price for that honor. Our diamonds are our diamonds, sir. Until they are no country's diamonds, the Secretary-General says. Is that a threat? No, sadly, just a fact . . . unless we can rally the world around the memory of order, everything will continue to disintegrate. I'll speak with my capital . . . there is no precedent for such a request, such an idea. Good show, France and the United Kingdom say, we must be reasonable these days. The Secretary-General nods. I understand your surprise; there is no precedent for any of this at all.

Later, in the small solitude of his bunk, the Secretary-General stares at a photograph of the New York headquarters taped to his wall. The Secretariat gleams aquamarine in the sunshine, the General Assembly curves alien and gold, Queens hangs in moth-eaten silhouette behind. All staff had been evacuated by the time the waters came. Swollen, the East River heaved up and pitched over the FDR Drive. It ripped chunks out of the cafeteria and swamped the library, flushing the archives out to the bay. The General Assembly hall and all its chambers remain an aquarium, fish peering at the grand Portinari murals, civilizations of algae sprouting from the Norwegian wood of the Security Council. In the Secretariat, however, the water never got any higher than the twelfth floor. A recovery team sent him reports of the surviving stories, their windows often blown out, mold and rust running through their veins, but otherwise the desks and offices in perfect order. The mysterious internal circuitry whirred in places. Engineers reported lights flickering and air coursing through the vents, the hum of a copy machine warming up. There was still breath in the building, stirring the beams as they leaned back and forth with the tides.

One treasure he was able to salvage before the catastrophe is a bust of the astronomer Copernicus, a gift from the Communist government of Poland in 1970, nearly a century ago. It is a bludgeoning work, the sullen face of the astronomer hewed from granite, emerging like a Neolithic god from its halo of rock. The Secretary-General keeps the bust in his room. He brings his fingers to his lips and then touches the monumental brow. Goodnight, Copernicus, he says.

Elsewhere on the MaidenX Orbital Hotel, diplomatic aides wait their turn to use the hotel's communications equipment. When MaidenX launched this facility into orbit, the company didn't want guests to spend time messaging home. Why be distracted from the luxury of the finest extraterrestrial cruise? Why trouble yourself with earthly matters when wined and dined among the stars? Nobody ever imagined that one day the hotel might host a global governing body, a guest that needed to be in touch with the earth in order to be in touch with itself. Its officers gather updates from ground staff; its mission representatives send cables to their capitals several times a day.

The business of running the world must carry on. There are frequent committee meetings and votes on the MaidenX. Recently, the council agreed unanimously to issue a decree urging all member states to fund desalination projects. This abundance of seawater must be turned into something usable. Other votes are more contentious. Norway complains about the raids of privateers from the Baltic Sea on its offshore oil rigs. She demands that sanctions be imposed upon the Baltic states. Only Latvia made it up to the MaidenX. What do you expect us to do, he says, we have no control over these pirates . . . we're just a small state, and in these times, the small state is even smaller than the non-state.

Queues snake down the hall from the cafeteria to the single computer lab, where Paraguay and Bolivia quietly catch up on their local football scores—the ball rolls on in the mountains. Kazakhstan leaves his screen, dejected. He hasn't received any message from his government. Maybe they've just forgotten about me, he thinks optimistically. France and the United Kingdom have long given up hope of hearing from their foreign ministries, if such things still exist. They play table tennis in the rec room. Sometimes, they ask for the 1g to be dialed down toward 0g. The amused MaidenX staff are happy to oblige. Every touch of the paddle on the ball sends France and the United Kingdom hurtling about the room. The weightless air becomes their surface, the memory of the floor their net; they execute backflips and cartwheels, plunging like seals for the irresistible ball.

In the bar, Mexico pours Luxembourg another whiskey. My government approves the Botswana proposal, he says. So would mine, I think. Were it all signed and sealed, would you want to stay in Gaborone or would you ask for a new post? I'm not sure there are other posts on offer! I'm going to be honest with you and say this: it would make me happy if you chose to stay on, if we could discover Gaborone together just as we have discovered life in space together. You are too sweet.

Mexico leans forward in his seat and clears his throat. Has anyone told you, he begins to say but stops, realizing that she is not paying attention. What is he doing? she asks. Mexico follows her gaze to Kiribati, pressing his head against a window, mouthing words, and counting on his fingers. I hope he's all right. Poor guy, Mexico says generously, he's got every reason to go mad. He walks over to Kiribati with his own whiskey outstretched. No thanks, Kiribati says with a smile before looking out again, we're facing Uranus, it's that blue dot, see? Uranus has twenty-seven moons. Yes, I know, Luxembourg says. She has joined them by the window. You can't see the moons, Kiribati continues, not with the naked eye of course, but you can imagine them there . . . They're named after Shakespearean spirits of the air . . . Titania, Oberon. Yes, Luxembourg says, also Puck, Ariel, Caliban . . . isn't that splendid? Splendid, Mexico says, splendid, splendid.

A little later, Botswana makes her way from the computer lab to the bunk of the Secretary-General. My government approves, she says to the blinking man in pajamas. We can settle down in Gaborone as soon as two weeks. What did they say about thirty-three percent? It'll be no more than twelve. Twelve. Yes. Okay, that will have to do, thank you. I'll make the announcement at the morning session.

The news comes as a relief to everybody, especially the owner of the MaidenX. His voice is projected into the council hall. Congratulations, he tells the ambassadors, best of luck in your new home. I hope you remember your time in the Orbital Hotel fondly. In a private phone call with the Secretary-General, he is less warm. I'm afraid your bills are grossly in arrears. The Secretary-General apologizes. As you can imagine, this is not the best time for our accounting people . . . we're a bit stretched, what with so many peacekeeping missions, innumerable refugee crises, famines, droughts, floods. We will give you a fortnight, but that is it, this jamboree has to come down to earth. It's not confirmed yet, Gaborone may not be ready in two weeks. Please appreciate that our hospitality is much sought after; there are organizations willing to remunerate us for the privilege and safety of near-earth orbit. Ours isn't just any old organization, you know, we carry the aspirations of the world. The world is down there, the owner says; on the MaidenX, you're just taking up space.

They hang up. The Secretary-General rubs the blunt nose of Copernicus. I shouldn't be so surprised, he says to the bust, nothing revolves around us anymore.

In the viewing vestibule, Kiribati plays with the imaging overlays on the windows. He zooms toward the star Rigel. The pixels resolve into the distant Witch Head nebula, a cloud of gas that looks like a sorceress mid-incantation. He delights in tracing its uncanny shape: the long devilish chin, the smoky tip of its nose, the recess of its eyes and pinched cheeks, its open mouth where other stars and other worlds are constantly being born.

A moaning from the opposite side of the vestibule distracts him. Kazakhstan is pulling at his hair. The lights have gone out in Astana. He pounds the unbreakable glass, made with such intelligent polymers that it doesn't even shiver at his anguish. The tears spill down his cheeks. If the room was taken down to 0g, they would lift off his face and he could bat them away, or he could surround himself in a cloud, make a fog out of his misery. There is no MaidenX staffer in sight, so Kazakhstan's tears fall at the same speed they would fall on the surface of the earth.

Kiribati puts an arm around his shoulders. There, there, he says, don't rush to conclusions. It could just be a power cut, a momentary thing . . . you can't surrender so easily. I haven't been able to get through to anybody at home. An electrical storm, a broken satellite, there are plenty of possible explanations. Look, Kazakhstan says, just look. The MaidenX bends toward the sun. A line of blue swells, then burns orange and red. Sunrise. Light sweeps over Eurasia and reveals a glittering silver stain. The ambassadors reckon with the tall cloud, distended by the wind, hanging over the irradiated silence of the steppes.

Astana has been bombed, Luxembourg tells Mexico in the cafeteria as he squeezes extra mustard on his hamburger. Another month, another bombing. Poor Kazakhstan . . . Who would have done it? I don't know, those bloody non-state actors are impossible to understand. It makes you wonder what the point is. Atrocity for the sake of atrocity, that kind of logic is always inscrutable. No, I mean, what the point is of grief. Of grief? If everybody is grieving, then grief loses its distinction, it just becomes a shared, permanent state. I suppose. So why do it? Because grieving is helpless, because how else do you respond to loss? I don't see Kiribati grieving. Kiribati is going insane. No, I disagree . . . his country literally no longer exists, so it makes sense that all he can do is look at the stars, the planets, the depths of space. You think that's healthy? I'd rather explore the cosmos than feel sorry for myself. There are other things we can do to hide from our losses. You're going to suggest that we go dancing. Correct, Mexico says. Luxembourg laughs. I'm a terrible dancer. That's okay . . . in zero G, there's no such thing as bad dancing.

In the room that they share with Kenya and Jordan, Kiribati gives Kazakhstan a cup of tea. The ambassador tries to take a sip but puts the mug aside. No more, no more, he says, my country is no more. From the cubby by his bed, Kiribati removes an old coffee tin. Close your eyes and hold this, he says. Kazakhstan does as he is told. Jordan puts a consoling hand on Kazakhstan's wrist while Kenya sits cross-legged on the floor, listening to Kiribati.

We knew for many years that our islands were doomed, that the ocean would take them . . . but we thought it would happen gradually: an atoll here and there, a beach eaten away, until the sea seeped into our groundwater and made life impossible. Then the day came . . . I was already up in the MaidenX so I've only heard the stories and seen some of the videos . . . They say it was difficult to know what was what, to tell the tsunami from the storm, that it seemed like an unbroken mass of water and wind rising to the roof of the sky. Dreadful, Kenya shakes his head. Jordan says something grave, one assumes along the same lines. Only with satellite imaging, Kiribati says, can you see the outlines of my underwater islands, faint like a footprint, the suggestion of a country no longer there.

He opens the tin in Kazakhstan's lap. I collected this several years ago and I'm blessed for my foresight . . . This is what I have left of my home. Into an empty mug he pours out half of the fine white sand. Keep it, he tells Kazakhstan, let it help you be at home as it helps me.

Kazakhstan stares for a while into the depths of the mug and then looks wordlessly at Kiribati. The four ambassadors share a communicative kind of silence, where each feels somehow yoked to the others, as if they were melting together in this floating oven in the void, before Jordan breaks the quiet with loud sobs and a speech, spluttering in untranslated sound what they had already felt in its absence.

In the following days, Mexico and Luxembourg make it a habit of slipping away to the dance studio when nobody else is there. They have the room sealed and the artificial gravity turned off.

Mexico allows Luxembourg to choose the music that plays on their headphones. He finds that her tastes are eclectic to the point of incoherence. She pulls up old swing albums followed by Indonesian gamelan. They fumble from wall to wall, unable to find a beat. She puts on French techno and they split apart, shaking about on their own. When he intervenes and tries to control them into the movements of a pop ballad, she grows impatient. She switches to a Balkan Gypsy dance, all bellowing brass and soaring vocals, which she sings herself. The lyrics, she tells him as they spin around and around, are about the power of moonlight.

On one occasion, they find France and the United Kingdom already inside. The older men float serenely in a waltz. They are only too happy for Mexico and Luxembourg to join. The four ambassadors wheel around the room in alternating pairs, trying to imitate the waltz's drifting grace without the counterpoint of the floor. Mexico is grateful for the change of pace. When he waltzes with Luxembourg, they tether their hips together, and she lets him lead her. They spin slowly, revolving on an easy axis that he maintains with effort, at times parallel, at times perpendicular to the ground. Mexico searches for Luxembourg's eyes, tries to hold their gaze, but she is smiling at him, away from him, over his shoulder and out of the room, into empty regions beyond.

The last time they dance together, he floats her to the wall during a reggaeton song. He holds her there, too purposefully perhaps, but she does not resist. When they kiss, the tiny force of their lips pushes them away from each other and he must grab hold of her belt. They do not kiss again. Luxembourg asks for the gravity to be restored and they slide down to the floor. I'm sorry, she tells him, I can't—no part of me can . . . even my desires feel weightless.

In a private council, Botswana meets with the Secretary-General to deliver updates about progress in Gaborone. Suitable workspaces have been made for all the officers of the Secretariat. Temporary accommodation is being built, with long-term plans for permanent structures. As far as the missions are concerned, it's unclear how many countries will be able to maintain delegations, but for the time being there is enough office space to fit—in close quarters—nearly a hundred embassies. Gloomily, the Secretary-General admits that number should be more than enough. Offices and residences will be so close that no mission will need to keep a car; everything will be walking distance. We'll have finally gone green, the Secretary-General says. Food trucks and soup kitchens will roll in during lunch and dinner times. I must tell Kazakhstan, Botswana says, that we've even found a chef who can make Adana kebabs. She laughs, but then realizes her mistake. The Secretary-General corrects her anyway. If Kazakhstan chooses to join us in Gaborone—and he may not—it will probably be as an observer and a friend, not a member.

Kiribati is eating dessert in the cafeteria. The surface of Saturn's moon Titan, he tells Kazakhstan, is viscous with a paper-thin crust . . . if you took a spoon to it, it would crack just like this crème brûlée. They tap the surface of their puddings and watch the amber shards lift against each other like tectonic plates. Kiribati carries on. Titan's lakes resemble tar pits, all great expanses of sludge . . . a boat trying to sail across would not get very far . . . near the equator, you would think that little changes, that wind is an unknown concept on Titan . . . but there is tremendous weather closer to the poles . . . cyclones stir the Kraken Sea into a whirlpool of methane, benzene falls like snow in blizzards. Have you ever seen snow? Kazakhstan asks. Yes, I have in fact. Where? In New York, my first and only year as head of mission. How was it? Lovely . . . I took so many pictures of snow falling in front of streetlamps, snow hanging in the trees, snow collected in the creases of jackets, snow on fire escapes . . . even after it all melted, little pyramids of snow survived on my balcony and I let them grow black. That must have all been such a strange sight for you, coming from your sunny paradise. Actually no, Kiribati says, it was exactly as I imagined.

In his room, the Secretary-General reports to Copernicus. We have lost touch with five separate peacekeeping and peacemaking missions in the past week . . . they've been overrun, or obliterated, or bribed to disperse, or, worst of all, they've just given up and abandoned their positions. Copernicus grimaces. I'm told that there are refugee camps with no doctors, no medicines, no security, no tents . . . why even call them camps, they're just collections of refugees festering in the sun. Where are we? Copernicus asks with dry lips. Too far away, much too far away from where we should be . . . we came up here for safety, but this remove is maddening . . . we need to be in the thick of things, to be seen, to be believed in. Earth, Copernicus says, that's where it's at. We'll be set up in Gaborone in a matter of days. I've never been south of the equator before. You'll be planted there soon and, who knows, maybe it will be for a long time, for the rest of time. What fun . . . just let me be in the sun. Goodnight, Copernicus. Goodnight.

The meteorologists begin sounding alarms the next day. Thanks to the warming of the southern Atlantic, large storms in the horse latitudes are increasingly common. One such depression brews near the battered coasts of South Africa. The ambassadors watch its formation from the viewing vestibule. It grows as it drifts east, the storm bands swollen, tufting like beaten egg whites. This is going to make for a tricky landing, Luxembourg says. Full of whiskey, Mexico shrugs. I've seen worse. But in the following hours, the storm gains the width of a country, the breadth of a continent. Meteorologists calculate that at its heart the wind churns at over 250 kilometers per hour. A ridge of high pressure from the north fixes the storm over Namibia and it grinds east over the desert, untamed by wind shear, monstrous in its ghostly scrawl.

Botswana cannot bring herself to watch the eye of the storm pass over Gaborone. Lightning explodes in blue bursts through the clouds. Mexico feels Luxembourg's fingers entwining his own. Don't worry, he whispers, it will dissipate soon . . . no storm can last long overland. She shivers. That storm is a thousand times the size of my country . . . it looks like the end of the world. Not the world, Kiribati says, but the end of a world, just another such end. Mexico notices then that Luxembourg's other hand is wrapped around Kiribati's wrist. He lets her fingers drop.

Eventually, after many attempts, a weak message gets through to the MaidenX. Gaborone is no longer in any shape to play host.

The Secretary-General calls the owner of the MaidenX. Listen, what can we do, we've nowhere else to go. I, too, saw the storm. Please be reasonable, nobody could have predicted it. Indeed. We need to explore our options, just let us stay up here for a little longer. In that case, we have to make some overdue cuts, some necessary economizing. Like what? No more champagne. Fine. Hot water available only for half the day. I suppose we can get used to the occasional cold shower. And do you have any idea how expensive it is to generate artificial gravity? I imagine it's quite costly . . . Do you know how expensive it is to generate peace on earth? There will have to be enforced periods of 0g on board . . . beginning in a few hours.

In preparation for 0g, the staff of the MaidenX do their best to tie down all loose objects, to seal the tops of saltshakers, to make sure all the knives in the kitchen are secured in drawers.

But even they can't account for every object in the sprawling vessel. In the ad hoc council chamber, the nameplates of all the countries rise into the air, bobbing out of all logical sequence, the *As* with the *Ms*, the *Ks* with the *Vs*, observers mingling with member states. The bust of Copernicus bumps its head against the ceiling of the Secretary-General's room. Ouch, Copernicus says each time, waking the Secretary-General from his floating sleep. Kazakhstan and Mexico play doubles table tennis with France and the United Kingdom, though Mexico is resolutely frustrated in his attempt to keep score. Nobody apart from him seems interested. The Holy See chases after his rosary, which darts like a snake into the wilderness of the cafeteria. In the viewing vestibule, Kiribati and Luxembourg float hand in hand. If you light a candle in 0g, the flame doesn't taper, she says, but instead takes the form of a glowing sphere, a will-o'-the-wisp. Humans aren't meant for space, he replies, weightlessness eats away at our bones.

Before the MaidenX switched off artificial gravity, Kazakhstan had thoughtlessly placed the mug given to him by Kiribati inside a bedside-table drawer. He hadn't considered the tenacity of sand. It steams out of the cracks of his bedside table, forms a cloud over their bunk beds. The grains pull apart. Some drift in a fine mist down the hallways. Others float helplessly into the ventilation, to be circulated around the ship, slipping invisibly among the floating objects and people of the MaidenX. When the artificial gravity is restored, the sand falls to the floor, so diffused as to be imperceptible.

PORTRAIT WITH COAL FIRE

Hello! All I'm getting is a black screen.

But I see you. Hello?

There you go. Hello! What a pleasure this is. And hello to you, too, I assume you're helping him talk to me.

(Translator: Yes, he asked for my assistance in making the Skype call and speaking with you.)

Okay. Well, it's a thrill to reconnect. It's not often—well, almost never—that we have the chance to talk to those we photograph in the field again. I'll bring the rest of the staff in to say hi to you shortly.

You have a very beautiful office.

Thank you. It's not really mine, I'm just using it for the purpose of our conversation. Where are you speaking to me from? An Internet café?

You must be very busy . . .

Oh, no, for you, I have all day—

. . . so I don't want to take too much of your time. It was so good of you to send me a copy of the magazine.

Please, it was the least I could do. Many of my colleagues forget that we owe everything to people like you.

When the package came, the postman was so surprised. He'd never been to my street before. He had to knock on all the doors and ask for me by name.

I have to confess that I didn't know exactly how to write your address.

I don't, either! Anyway, you'll find this charming. I waited for all my family to wake up in the morning, and we opened the envelope together, pulled out the magazine, and put it on the middle of the table. What a beautiful thing.

Great.

We had such fun going through it. My children took turns, one by one, flipping through the pages. We marveled at all the pictures, the maps and animals and stars. Your magazine is so wondrous. We'd never seen a fish so big, longer than a man . . . What is it called?

(Translator: Tuna.)

Tuna. Every day, when she comes back from school, my daughter practices her English by reading that article on tuna.

I'd be overjoyed to send you a couple of cans of tuna.

You're always too kind. Sometimes, I'm embarrassed to say, I got confused and didn't realize that the advertisements were different from the other photos, but my wife is quite clever, and she could tell one from the other. These give the magazine money, she said, and these the magazine pays for. Women have such a better sense of how the world works.

Don't they just!

Then there was that picture of the cosmos, of those spots called black holes. My son put his fingers on it and said that it looked like bread hot and blistered off the stove. He thought it was amazing. These powerful telescopes can make the sky resemble roti.

I can introduce you to our science photo editor. Shall I bring him in?

Thank you. But please let me finish this story first, I've been thinking about it for some time and trying to keep it straight. And the Internet café might time out the connection.

Of course. I don't remember any Internet connections in your village or the neighboring ones.

Let me tell the story. By now, you see, our neighbors were already curious and poking their heads in and patting me on the back and even bringing me sweets, like there was some victory to celebrate.

How lovely.

Then we came to your piece. There were the pictures of villages and mines.

I should have said this before: it is so nice to see you again.

And we were awestruck, I tell you, completely wowed.

You've no idea how happy that makes me.

It was as if you had stepped behind our eyes and were seeing just as we saw our world. I was stunned. I don't know how you made the colors so real, even more than real. There is one photo of evening, of the coal fires burning, the blue walls of our houses, the dogs and people looking like black shapes in the smoke. I thought it was beautiful.

You're too kind.

Everybody else thought so, too. Each day when I come home from the mine, I take out my phone and try to make a picture like yours. They never come out well. Too dark, too gloomy. Here, see. So blurry. Please, show them to him.

(Translator: I'm messaging you these photos he has taken of his own village, inspired by your photos.)

Got them. I'm touched. I'm lucky to have a very expensive camera. That's the only difference.

No, no, don't be modest, you have a special skill. You have great imagination. I would never think to climb all the way down into a mine just to take a photo.

That was a very difficult shot. I thought I was going to die on the climb back, that the railings and ramp would give way any second. It's so impressive that you and so many other people do that trek every day, carrying loads of rock. It's just remarkable.

It's not remarkable, it's what we do.

Ah, so you see, you may think my work is astonishing, but I also think that what you do is astonishing.

Do you?

Yes. That's one of the reasons I had such feeling for you and your family. Forgive the analogy, I know this is a stretch, but in many ways, my work is similar to yours. I, too, have to go into the mine. For long, dark, lonely hours, I chip away at the coalface. When I come back to the surface, I have thousands of images, the way you bring up so many lumps of coal. Just like you, I spend so much time sorting them, making various piles based on their quality. In the end, my photos are shipped off and consumed by big companies and family households.

I'm not understanding.

(Translator: He's saying that taking pictures is like mining coal.)

I see. I suppose you're right, in some ways.

Sorry, it's just a metaphor. I don't have to breathe in coal dust, I don't have to live in all that smoke.

I found a plastic sleeve for the magazine. We keep it wrapped up and under my pillow during the night. I don't want the pictures to fade.

I can get you as many extra copies as you want. Just say the word, and we'll ship them to you.

I don't need any more copies, we already have ours. As I was saying, we all marveled at the images of the village and the mines. There was a man in some other place you went to, standing with his cart deep in the mine, and all the lines on his face and body were swollen and gray, like he was made of rock, and I said to my family, This is exactly it, the more time we spend in the mines, the more we become part of the mines. Your pictures show that.

Thank you. It's wonderful to hear your reactions to the work.

My daughter finally turned the page and when I saw it, my immediate reaction was to pick up the magazine and lift it straight to my face, so that I was the first one to look at the picture.

That's not very generous of you. You should let them share in the moment!

I brought it so close to my face that I could only see myself in parts, so I had to put it back down in front of everybody. They were quiet for a second and then they burst out laughing. It didn't look like me at all.

I'm sorry. I try to keep all my work as natural as possible.

No, what I mean is, it didn't look like how I looked like in photos.

Yes, that's what I mean.

It's odd to see yourself in a magazine, it's difficult.

But it must also be a thrill, no?

I've looked at the photo so many times now. Each time, I see something new. For instance, there is a man on the left-hand side, right at the edge, in a red plaid shirt, just standing and watching.

I'm not sure I remember.

He's covered by the smoke, but you can see him if you look very closely. I don't know who he is, maybe one of the assistants you brought into the village.

My assistants?

(Translator: One of your fixers.)

Anyway, I realized only recently, maybe after the thousandth time looking at the photo, that the stranger is smiling. You can see his teeth, even behind all that smoke.

Smiling.

Yes. And I wondered, Why is he smiling? What is this man

smiling about? Nothing that I'm doing in the photo should make anybody smile. I'm stoking a fire that has to burn hot for six hours for the coal to turn into coke, which we need for our house and to sell in the market. I explained all that to you. You see me in the photograph, I'm in pain. The heat is so intense. My eyes are closed, I'm bent over, reaching with the poker in one hand, shielding myself from the flames with another. My clothes are filthy after a long day's work, my turban dark with sweat and dust. I'm grimacing and my mouth is open, and you can see my gray lips, my thin bloody teeth.

Yes, I don't know how you could stand the heat. I was several feet away taking the photo and my hands were burning even there.

And this stranger in the photo is smiling at your camera. Why was he smiling?

I don't know. Sometimes people do strange things in front of cameras, things they don't mean to do. I just take the photos, I don't make the people do anything.

Were you smiling?

Of course not. Is this smiling man the problem?

I'm ugly in this picture. I'm supposed to look ugly. That's why the man in the red shirt is smiling. Because he knows he's better than me.

No.

He's wearing a clean shirt. His teeth are white. Is that what people will do when they see this picture of me? Smile and feel better about themselves?

No. Not at all. I reject that. Maybe, if it was up to me, I wouldn't have picked this exact picture of you. But you are not hideous in this photograph. If anything, our readers will look at it and think with admiration about your strength, your perseverance.

You took so many photos, I watched you, so many. Why did you choose this one?

I didn't choose it. My editor did.

Why did you let your editor choose this one?

Do you want to talk to her? I can bring her into this office.

I don't want to talk to her. I don't know her. I know you.

She chose the photo, I only gave her suggestions.

So you suggested it. Why did you suggest it?

It captures a very real moment in your day. It shows you in the midst of your labor. If you want to know, I also thought the coal fire cast a very striking orange light on your body, a light that sparked in the dullness of the smoky landscape, the sad trees, the low houses, the pantsless children standing watch.

Listen, it doesn't matter to me what my neighbors say. It doesn't matter that they make jokes about me now, that they say I'm famous around the world for being a dirty miner, that I'm making the rest of them look bad. They've always been jealous of my family and my happiness. What upsets me is the way my children look at the photo. I don't like them seeing me that way.

They know who you are, they know what you do. They shouldn't think any less of you.

I hope so, but you're not in a position to know that.

No, that's true, I'm not.

Your magazine is amazing. It teaches us things we didn't know about, like the way ice moves, the ancient ships you find in the mud of your rivers, the Indians of your country and how they love their horses, take pride in their horses.

Yes, we have our own Indians.

But your photo made me part of this big world, no? This other place. For my children, the picture is becoming their image of me. Whoever I was before and whoever I am now are less real to them. It's like my life is less real than the picture.

Don't be silly.

They look at me now at home, at dinner, in the morning, like I'm somebody else.

Please don't cry. Why are you crying?

(Translator: Give him a second.)

Excuse me. I love my daughter, she is my biggest hope in life. Do you know what she told me recently? She came to me and she said, Papa, why don't you have a name?

A name?

(Translator: Yes, a name.)

Why would she say that?

A name. My daughter said, In the magazine, Papa, lots of other people in the photos have names. Some of the animals have names. Even the stars and galaxies have names, and they're just purple and black and white shapes. But you don't have a name. The magazine calls you a "miner" or "a man" or "the man" or a "coal tender."

But we didn't use your name.

Right.

Forgive me, I understand why this would upset you. What can I say? These kinds of decisions are above my pay grade. I provide the photos, but I don't get to write the captions. I would say that this was just company policy, but to be honest with you, with the way things are going in the industry, with the morale in the office, I just don't know what company policy is these days.

I'm not understanding. You knew my name. You knew my family mattered more to me than tending the coal fires.

Of course. That's why I went out of my way for you. Don't you remember?

Yes. I'm so grateful for our family portrait.

It wasn't easy finding a print shop in your district. I spent a full day on the road looking for one that was open and had functioning equipment. I did it for you because I cared, because I admired you, because I wanted the best for you and your family always. Please believe that. I even made sure I got it framed.

It is a beautiful picture. You captured all of us perfectly. The way my daughter has her arm around my son. The way my wife holds the end of her yellow dupatta. Over my shoulder, you can see a little bit inside our home, you can see the shrine we keep, the pictures of our family gods. I've just had my morning bath and I'm wearing a clean lungi, my hair is parted to the side. I'm proud and I'm smiling.

You've memorized it. I'm touched.

I brought it with me. I'm lifting it up to the camera. Can you see it? Just look at this wonderful picture. This is something beautiful that you made.

Thank you. Look at them. They're gorgeous.

I'd like the magazine to print it in a future issue.

Publish this photo?

Yes.

That's a lovely idea, but I'm sorry, I can't make any promises. To be honest, I don't think we'll be able to do that.

Why?

Again, I can bring in the editors, and they can explain to you how it works.

You can explain it to me.

We don't publish posed photographs like this unless we have a real reason to, unless they're part of some kind of series. The editors probably don't plan to revisit the subject of coal mines in your region anytime soon. You have to understand that a lot of thought, debate, argument, and competition goes into deciding what's in the magazine. There's very little I can do. In the grand scheme of things, I'm just small fry.

Only a little fish? You're not like tuna.

Right. From my part as well, this is not the kind of photography I do. I capture the world as it happens. My hope is that my camera eliminates the barrier between the viewer and the subject, that the viewer is brought right into the image.

(Translator: He's saying that he wants his photos to look like he isn't there.)

Does that make sense? I don't normally take posed photos like that one. My work strives for a kind of naturalness.

It's not unnatural, it's my family.

Of course, but you do understand what I mean? I'm sorry, I don't want to give you false hope.

Please publish it. I'd like my family to see ourselves this way.

Why don't you talk to the editors?

I don't know them, I know you. This is the magazine you sent me. Yes, it's a bit worn, it's been thumbed through many times.

If only all our issues were this well-read.

This is the photo of me. There is the strange man smiling. Look, you can see him if you hold the magazine closer to your face. Why is he smiling?

I don't know.

On the same page, what do you see? Above the photo of me? What is this?

It's a photo of me.

A black-and-white little square with your face. You are showing your straight teeth. You are smiling. Isn't this what you call posed? Is it natural?

It's my profile photo. It's different.

What's this written here?

(Translator: "Hugh Bellerin.")

That's my name.

Your name.

Okay. I understand if you feel used. I'm more than aware of these pitfalls of my profession. Sometimes, we can be rightfully accused of exploiting our subjects. I know that I have power over your representation, that our relationship is completely asymmetrical. I try to treat this imbalance delicately. Maybe this is a glaring example of that difficulty, of the ethical dangers of what I do. I feel dreadful, really. But I did this work because I thought your life, your world, your story was important. If you feel insufficiently compensated for that recognition, I'm sure we can address that.

I'm not understanding.

(Translator: He's saying that the magazine can give you money.)

I don't want money. That's not what I'm asking for. Please publish the picture of my family. It's your picture anyway, you took it with your own hands.

Please understand, there are some things that are just not in my power. Let's talk to the editors. Just wait a second, I'll bring them into the conversation.

I don't mean to be rude, but these editors don't owe me anything. Why should they help me?

Listen. I'm trying to be fair. I could have submitted photos of you drinking, of you asleep outside the toddy shop. I didn't do that. My best photograph from the entire trip was a picture of you draped over a trough of moonshine, covered in mud and booze, a pig sniffing at your fingers.

I'm not a drunk.

You know what I did with that photograph? I deleted it. Nobody will ever have the chance to see it.

You haven't lived my life.

I understand. I don't blame you. Nobody would.

That was a terrible thing to do, to take a photo like that.

Yes, it was. But it would have been an even more terrible thing to publish it, wouldn't it?

(Translator: Please, there is no need to raise your voice. He's speaking with great civility.)

I'm sorry, I didn't mean to yell. There's only so much I can do for you. It must cost you a day's wage, maybe more, just to have this talk with me.

(Translator: More, he also has to pay for my services.)

Right, I worry that you're doing all this in vain.

You came all the way to me, now I've come to you. I treated you with kindness in my home. Please treat me with kindness too.

I don't understand. What's he saying?

(Translator: The world is so unequal, but sometimes we can make it less so.)

Okay. It is really an honor to see you again. A privilege. Why don't I bring my editor in and let her decide?

Will she understand why that man in my photo is smiling?

No, she won't be able to explain that.

If you won't give me your assurance that the photograph will be published, she won't either. I know how accountability works. The further you are from the mine, the less responsible you become for what happens there.

This isn't a mine, it's the office of a magazine.

(Translator: Why don't you just accept the photograph? Tell him you'll have it published. That'll appease him.)

But it was just a gift.

(Translator: The poor guy is going to have to skip a few meals to make up for this call.)

I'm not going to lie to him, he's taken all this expense.

(Translator: All the more reason for you to let him leave feeling happy.)

What are you talking about? Please. Take the photograph of my family. My friend will send you a scanned version now. Publish it.

Okay. We'll take it then. How can I say no?

Really?

(Translator: I'm sending you a hi-res scan of the photo.)

Yes. We'll run it. I'll do what I can to make sure it gets into the magazine. Maybe we can even publish a little interview about you and your family.

Just the photograph, please. Thank you. You are a decent man.

Not as decent as you.

My daughter has written each of our names for you, here, so you can put the correct caption next to the picture.

(Translator: These are your names?)

Yes.

(Translator: There seems to be a little problem.)

Why don't you bring that piece of paper to the camera so I can see it, too?

What's wrong? She told me she wrote our names in American letters so that you could read them.

I'm sorry, these aren't your names. Tell him what the girl has written.

(Translator: This is what it says: Phytoplankton, Nebula, Carbon, Tuna.)

THE MIRRORS OF ISKANDAR

PREFACE

Each of these short pieces springs from an episode of "the Alexander romance," a cycle of stories about Alexander the Great. Beginning in the fourth century A.D. (many centuries after the conqueror's death), the romance spread outward from the Levant. It was popular as far west as Scotland (condensed in medieval literary form in *The Buik of Alexander*) and as far east as the Straits of Malacca (the Malay epic *Hikayat Iskandar Zulkarnain*). The Alexander romance was global literature before global literature, an extraordinary example of the migration of fables, tropes, and histories through folklore and text.

Modern understandings of Alexander's life—which hew closely to the accepted historical record—have buried these more legendary accounts. But the purpose of the romance was never to tell a straightforward history. Its stories offered variously a vision of ideal kingship and courtly behavior; a cautionary tale about arrogance and ambition; prophetic revelations; a description of fantastical adventures; and a sense of the deep, conflicted past of the world as well as its fundamental impermanence.

The figure of Alexander as a Muslim hero—referred to as Iskandar, Sikandar, or Zul-Qarnain (the "two-horned one")—was developed by Arab and Persian writers, most famously the twelfth-century poet Nizami Ganjavi in his *Iskandarnamah* (the Book of Alexander). The Delhi poet Amir Khusrau produced his own version of the tale, known as the *Aina-ye-Iskandari* (the Mirror of Alexander), which contains a remarkable description of Alexander's submarine exploration of the depths of the sea. A few centuries later, Mughal artists in Akbar's atelier conjured in delicate miniature the finest paintings of the Alexander romance.

The following sequence builds on such texts and images.

I. THE DUEL OF THE ARTISTS

Along with the rest of his enormous entourage, Iskandar came to China with artists. They were practiced in all the styles of his lands—in the big cheeks of Rum, in the dusty eyebrows of the Persians, in the grain of Mesopotamia, in the delighted paunches of the Indians. The khan of China welcomed the great conqueror and his retinue. As usual, there was much feasting and drinking, belching and puking. For the first time in his life, Iskandar tried the famous Chinese numbing pepper and felt his tongue disappear. This is extraordinary, he said, what an amazing taste. The khan nodded. Is it true, the khan asked, that your mother had such bad breath your father had to return her? Steam and smoke rose from platters of meat. Acrobats tumbled between the tables. That's the story, Iskandar replied, I wouldn't know . . . no breath smells bad to me if its words are fair.

The next day, Iskandar called for a competition. Let us see which people are superior, he said to the khan. He set the terms of a wager. If the Chinese won out, then he would return west and leave the khan and his property unmolested. If my people prove the stronger, Iskandar said, well, you can imagine what'll happen next.

The tournament began. First, the javelin throwers sent spears whistling into the sky. Then the archers tested their precision, aiming for a glass cup, the fruit on a tree, the moving tail of a bullock. Wrestlers slapped their shoulders and rubbed their chests with soil. Sprinters became shadows on the steppes. Iskandar inspected the proceedings with a falcon latched to his wrist.

In all these feats, the Chinese were equal to his men. Nothing could separate the talents of the musicians either, nor the dancers. Philosophers got entangled in the logic of the other. The astrologers compared their catalogues of stars and planets and found that while they might see different forms in the sky, the substance was much the same. The calligraphers fell in love with each other's penwork, staying up all night to trace words in the sand and sentences in silk. They went to sleep dreaming in alien lines.

Finally, it was the turn of the artists. They were brought to a large rock cave. A curtain was placed in the middle, cutting the cave in half. They were given three days to compose a masterpiece. At the end of the three days, the curtain would be drawn and the artwork compared.

Iskandar's artists spent the first day preparing their paints. On the second day, they turned the rock face into a sprawling courtly scene: first, they painted the landscape in the background, mountains and waterfalls swaying in the torchlight; then they drew animals and peasants beyond the walls of the city; next came the rings of the city itself, its assemblies of merchants and soldiers, courtesans, vegetable sellers, butchers and drovers; then the marble pavilions of the court, their filigree and gold gleam. At the top of the court, lording over the entire scene, sat the turbaned form of Iskandar, back erect, placid-faced, watching as the khan bent over and rolled a set of dice.

Iskandar's artists spent the third day painting the hair, eyebrows, mustaches, and sideburns of every figure in their mural. At the end, they placed eyelashes on the goats and deer.

When Iskandar entered the cave, he laughed with pleasure at the sight of the mural. Nothing could surpass this accomplishment. No Chinese artist could match the deftness of color and movement, the pathos in the fall of each bit of clothing or each downturned gaze, nor the wonder of painting rock upon real rock, imbuing the stone with magical life. Iskandar called out to the khan. Draw the curtain, he said, and you'll see the end of your kingdom.

The curtain was drawn. Torchlight filled the cave. Iskandar couldn't believe it. The Chinese had painted the exact same mural. There were all the animals and men, walls and mountains, domes and minarets. He came closer and watched the Chinese mural sway and tremble, saw his shadow interrupt the painting.

It was a reflection. The Chinese artists had shaved and polished the wall to such a fine degree that the rock assumed the quality of a mirror. While your men were busy picking colors and sketching shapes, the khan said, mine transformed the cave itself. The khan ordered the curtain to be pulled forward. Iskandar watched the mural vanish from the wall. Naked stone stretched before him, alive with its own dark light.

He stayed with the khan for another week. Afterward, reprovisioned and laden with gifts, Iskandar and his entourage returned home.

2. SURVEILLANCE

Iskandar received news of attacks against his merchants in the Levant. Soon after they went out to sea, pirates from Cyprus would seize them. The raids were costly. Iskandar was furious when he learned that pirates had intercepted a finely dappled mare intended for his mother in Macedonia. He mourned for the poor horse now alone in some piratical hold, surrounded by the treasures and sundries of the sea.

Why can't they be stopped? he asked Aristotle. They're so elusive, the sage said, nobody can find pirates who hide in the foam and spray. Can't we just conquer Cyprus and get it over with? My lord, we've done the calculations and it seems clear that Cyprus is just not worth the capital investment of its conquest. But I'm a world conqueror, what will people say if after all this time I haven't taken Cyprus? You are a world conqueror, my lord, and the world is entirely yours . . . A world without Cyprus is still very much the world.

Iskandar relented. Instead of dispatching an expeditionary force to Cyprus, he sent his architects and engineers from the east to construct an enormous tower. It loomed over the coast, wide at the base, narrowing like a ziggurat after each level till its gleaming pinnacle.

A series of lenses and mirrors was fixed to the top. Sentries peered through this telescope, searching the waters for pirates.

At the first sight of an enemy ship, the guards waved flags alerting the merchant vessels below. Iskandar's own warriors would push out to sea and chase the corsairs. The men on the tower watched as the ships neared each other, as puffs of smoke from the guns drifted over the waves, as the oars fenced and the hulls bumped. Combat is silent through a telescope. When muted against the sea, the sight of men flailing on blood-slicked decks has all the drama of mime.

Soon, the pirates were defeated. Merchants sailed the eastern Mediterranean without cursing Cypriot mothers. Iskandar's own mother loved the horses he sent her. The telescopic tower developed other uses. Guards inspected incoming ships to determine which they'd steal from in the name of the law. They trained the telescope on processions of nuns, zooming in on their bare feet. Bored, they scanned the clouds for evidence of vaporous habitation. They even tried to probe the night sky and see what kindling burned beneath the stars.

In later years, before other conquerors cannibalized its stone, the tower cast its shadow on open pasture. Shepherds let their goats graze around its ruin as they stretched out on the grass and took in the view of the sea. Once, a shepherd boy was brave enough to test the tower's ghosts. He climbed to the top. There, he found the assemblage of glass and metal that had once been the telescope. It was cracked and rusted. He turned it this way and that. No matter how the boy looked into the object, he only saw a splintered reflection of his own face.

3. REFLECTIONS WHILE RAFTING

During the early weeks of each spring, the army was assembled for the year's campaign. Iskandar and his retinue had little to do but wait. Worse, they were stuck at court. Hunting was always disappointing in that time. The forests were scrawny, the animals scrawnier. Nature offered no threat, none of the abundant mystery that made heroes out of men on the chase.

One way to escape domestic tedium was to smoke hash and go rafting. While floating downstream, they watched the cormorants in conversation and imagined the feel of wind on their feathers. Aristotle assumed an animal spirit, posing on one leg like a stork, sticking his arms to the side. Tak tak tak tak tak tak, he said. The raft wobbled and Aristotle teetered into the water. Tak tak tak tak tak, he said as they dragged him up.

They told stories. Do you know what the ladies and gentlemen do for fun in Turkistan? one noble began. They go to the courtyard and have a long curtain strung up through the middle . . . the men go to one side and women to the other . . . at a certain point, they make a peephole, about waist level. I can guess where this is going, Iskandar said. Of course you can, the noble continued, but let me tell the others who are not as wise . . . Then the men in turns make themselves hard and stick their penises through the hole, and the women must guess whose penis it is.

That's the game? Yes, and everybody sings and plays instruments as it goes on.

I've heard a different version, Iskandar said. The women judge the penises . . . if they approve, they tie a ribbon around it. And if they dislike it? Well, if they find the penis ugly or think it has a malicious look, they tie a little bell to the tip, to make it look like a fool.

The nobles laughed. The stream widened and the current slowed. A convoy of silver fish plunged like daggers. After a silence, Iskandar spoke in a pensive tone. I'm feeling the world lightly, he said, so I'll share this sadness with you . . . Every time we conquer some place and we amass our loot, I take what gold we cannot carry and I bury it. That's nothing to feel sad about, a noble said, that's just prudent. I take two men with me to dig a hole, Iskandar continued, and then I kill them and bury them with the treasure. The nobles felt obliged to nod and grunt. I have to do this, Iskandar said. After all, wealth dissolves loyalty just as easily as it makes it . . . But sometimes, I think about how, when I'm gone, the entire world will be pockmarked with my secret gold and the bones of obedient men.

4. THE BARD'S TALE

With relish, Iskandar set about destroying Thebes. Battering rams on great wheels careened into the seven gates. Archers embroidered the parapets with iron. Engineers dug trenches to the foundations and set fires between the timbers and stones. Iskandar's cavalry uprooted the hinterland, scything down those peasants who hadn't yet run away to the forest, or climbed into the hills, or through some other provincial magic made themselves invisible to power. Ash hung in the air. When asked what he wanted to do with the city after its fall, Iskandar stared at the mountainous smoke and replied, What city?

Thebes's most famous bard fell at the feet of the conqueror. If you listen to my song, he said, you would know the wisdom of mercy. What instrument do you play? Iskandar asked. The flute. I hate the flute. Play the kamancheh instead. Luckily, the bard was skilled in many instruments besides the flute, including the daf, the barbat, and the kamancheh. Holding the kamancheh like a lamb, he sat down and began to sing.

He recalled the many tragedies of Thebes. In his boyish voice, they seemed more perverse than sad. A king confused for a wild animal and torn apart by his women, a warrior turned into a deer and eaten by his own dogs, Heracles driven so mad that he killed his own children, the crimes and misery of Oedipus, Tiresias divining fate like a farmer skimming cheese from milk. His prophecies went unheeded, the bard sang, but even now Tiresias tells the story of Thebes in the underworld, in words of black blood: this city is cursed, it is the end of ego, the end of power . . . By assaulting Thebes you make its story your own.

You have a nice voice, Iskandar said, but you misunderstand . . . I'm not assaulting Thebes, I'm destroying it. Anybody who thinks they can escape implacable fate, the bard said, will fail. That's the problem with Thebes . . . it won't recognize that I'm not just anybody.

Iskandar ordered the final advance. His men scampered over the walls, wrenched open the gates, and scoured the city with fire. The bard was bound to the parapets and made to watch the destruction. Pick up your instrument, Iskandar said. The bard played the kamancheh while the walls heaved, while the killing noise mingled with the lament of masonry, while the altar of Anahit and the altar of Heracles and the citadel of Cadmus came tumbling down, while Iskandar's marauders poured salt and rocks into the wells. Thebes shed its skin and cowered naked in its bits.

Before he left him, the conqueror reminded the bard of the creation myth of Thebes. When Amphion first raised your walls, Iskandar said, he played the kamancheh and sang, and his music bound the stones and mortar and plaster of your city. Tears slithered to the bard's lips. The kamancheh dropped from his hands. What music once did, Iskandar said, now music has undone.

5. MUSK DEER

Iskandar and his army happened upon the continental silence of Russia. When his soldiers came to the rare interruption of a town, they sacked it, clubbed the men, and added the women and children to the pens of slaves. Iskandar marveled at the emptiness of the country. Its trees stood so still. Its streams mourned beneath ice. His army marched on. They made their own landscape of sound, carpeting the taiga in brass and leather.

The siege of the Russian capital took only a few days. His men managed to pull down the stockades and sweep away the resistance. Iskandar allowed the ritual three days of pillage. By the middle of the first day, his men had run out of things to steal and people to rape. They turned to the palace of the Russian king. Normally, the loot of a royal residence was reserved for Iskandar. But it was only a shabby pile, a low stone structure with a long-beamed thatched roof, so he opened it up to his rank and file.

When they burst through the doors, they found a hall brimming with hundreds of musk deer. The smell was overpowering, and Iskandar's men struggled to press their way in. There were deer everywhere, chewing the tapestries, nursing fawns beneath the royal dais, defecating in the rushes, rutting against the boards, a whole civilization of deer jumbled in a warlord's hall. His soldiers uncovered a servant cowering in the cellar.

They asked him about the deer. The man looked at his toes. We thought you had come to Russia for the perfume of our musk deer, he said, so we hid them here. Hid them? We emptied the forests, the man said, we thought that if the conqueror doesn't find any of these deer, he won't bother with Russia . . . he'll just leave us alone.

6. THE LATITUDE OF NUSHABAH

For some time, Iskandar's favorite wife was Nushabah. He won her north of Khurasan and spent an autumn with her in Gilan. They were married when he settled her in Barda, near the Caspian Sea. He renovated a large garden home, stuffed it with all the luxuries of the known world. She was fond of astronomy, so he constructed an observatory in the lawns. After dinner, the couple spent time together alone. Nushabah would search the night sky and record the positions of stars and planets. Iskandar studied her and tried to write poems. He'd get distracted by her rigor, the plodding way she took notes, the repetitive turn of her jaw and chin, and soon he would be kissing her neck. They'd have sex, and afterward he let her trace the muscles beneath his chest hair. What's the point, Nushabah would say, don't go to war.

Iskandar could never be confused for a romantic. Love for him was an arena. Like war, it had its pageantry, its rules of engagement, its rewards and spoils. He knew nobody could match his prowess, but he still had to go through the motions of the contest. Sometimes, a victory filled him with a passion that seemed far larger than the moment itself. That feeling would pass. For each territory he conquered, he had several concubines and at least one wife. He loved them as kings must, as he loved a well-planed road or a strategic watchtower, all embodiments of his sovereignty over land and people. Yet with Nushabah alone the clamor of war receded. The stars and their quiet stretched without end.

The spring thaw approached. Advisors came to Iskandar with updates on the muster, the recruitment of mercenary light cavalry, the state of provisions. He waved them away. Later, later, not now. At the festival to mark the beginning of the new year, Nushabah and he leapt over the fire together, offering the darkness inside them to the flames. In the following weeks, generals told him about grumbling in the camps, about how the men itched to go on campaign. It's not time yet, Iskandar said. He completed a poem for Nushabah and read it aloud to her one night. She grabbed the page. You march all over the world, she laughed, but you can't write one straight line.

Spring edged into summer. Aristotle pulled Iskandar to his feet. Your time is short, the sage said. Everybody's time is short, Iskandar replied. Conquerors have even less time, and you are wasting it. This isn't wasting time . . . this is exactly how time should be spent. It's how men spend time. Yes, it is. Aristotle arched an eyebrow. Aren't you more than a man?

Iskandar told Nushabah it was the season of war and that he had to leave Barda. She was incredulous. Why fight this year? Just take a break for once, she said. If we don't campaign, he explained, then my enemies will think that I've weakened . . . they'll redouble their efforts against me. Which enemies? The Turanians. I thought you defeated them ages ago. I did, but they always need defeating. Anybody else? The Chinese. But they're so far away. Women have a different understanding of distance than men. Oh, do we. I also have to worry about the heathen Greeks, the restless Dacians, conspirators in my own camp, Indians who don't want to pay tribute, the Amazons raiding for young men, the giants eating our sheep. These problems will remain no matter what you do. Stop protesting . . . it doesn't make any difference for us anyway . . . your tent will be closest to mine and I promise to visit you four days out of seven.

Nushabah held his face in her hands, stroking the temples. I'm not coming with you. What? I'm going to stay right here. You can't do that. Of course I can . . . isn't this my home? You're my wife, you'll go where I tell you to. Against my will? Yes, even if it's against your will. I don't think you'll want me near you if it's against my will.

Iskandar considered her face, its honest resolve. Some of his women plucked their eyebrows every day before he came to them, but Nushabah seemed to do it only once a month. Little hairs crept above her nose. Does your army march in a straight line parallel to the equator? she asked. No, he said, it's an army, not a road. So I can't come, I need to see out the year in Barda . . . if you make me leave this latitude now, my astronomical observations will only be partial. So? If you must complete your work, that's fine . . . but won't you let me complete mine?

The evening after Iskandar and his army left Barda, Nushabah went to her observatory. She found it full of flowers and honeyed sweets. Strewn everywhere were crumpled bits of paper, all the aborted couplets that Iskandar had written for her and could never throw away.

Some months later, a messenger reached Iskandar on campaign. Varangian raiders had come down the rivers. They sacked Barda and torched the palace complex, the observatory included. Nushabah was gone. No one could tell Iskandar if the Varangians had taken her or if she had been left to burn in her home. The astrologers gave various explanations for the calamity, but whenever Iskandar looked to the stars, he found them illegible.

7. IN THE EYES OF A QUEEN

Before he conquered a new country, Iskandar would sometimes visit its king disguised as a messenger. This way he could judge for himself the ruler's manner, the spirit of his courtiers, the resolve that might make invasion difficult. Iskandar also enjoyed the acting. Claiming to be his own envoy, he appeared at the court of the king of Andalusia. He was welcomed with typical courtesies and brought into the royal audience, only to discover that the king of Andalusia was actually the queen of Andalusia. She was skinny by the standard of monarchs and had round eyes that glowed like coins. Unfazed, Iskandar delivered the normal blustering message. She smiled and then invited him to her private quarters.

This was not the normal way to treat messengers, but Iskandar had to obey. What does she want from me? he thought. He felt an unfamiliar nervousness, sweat on his palms and neck. When they reached her private wing, she dismissed the attendants. He looked around for a window or a weapon. Don't worry, she said, I know who you are. I'm but the humble messenger of my lord Iskandar, Iskandar said. Oh please, stop with that preposterous voice—you're the great conqueror, the man we all fear. That is a very strange idea. Not as strange as that beard you're wearing.

The queen pulled him into a side room full of paintings.

Each was a portrait of him. Your real facial hair is much better trimmed than this, she said, and ran her fingers through his fake beard. Iskandar stared at the depictions on the wall, the framed images leaning against chairs and desks. There he was on horseback in a green caftan. There he sat on his imperial dais receiving tribute from the Yemenis. There he consulted with Aristotle in the sage's cave. There he punished the heathen Greeks. There he was hunting, admiring falcons, supervising the design of cannons, sharing a cup of wine with a slave, glass-eyed watching a military parade, resting cross-legged beneath a tree fat with apricots, pardoning criminals on a Friday. I know who you are, the queen said, my spy in your court is a painter . . . he sends me these images of you as his reports.

Are you going to kill me? Iskandar asked. Prayers in twelve languages rebounded through his head. Even if I killed you, the queen said, your army would still cause problems for me and my people . . . so no, I won't, but we'll make a deal . . . you will accept provisions and safe passage through my lands, and in return you will leave in peace. Iskandar sighed. I accept. One more thing, the queen said, you will stand perfectly still as I paint you. Dressed like this? Exactly like this.

Iskandar had no choice. The queen produced an easel and canvas. He stood motionless for her in his shabby messenger's outfit, trying to form his false eyebrows into a dignified line. At the end, she showed him the work. He flinched at the shameful blush on his cheeks, the beard slipping off his jaw, his hands clenched in front of him, the expression of his eyes like those of a guilty teenager. Don't I have a deft brush? the queen asked. Doesn't it look just like you?

8. THE WATER OF LIFE

Iskandar brought his army to the Land of Darkness. The enormous mountain Qaf blocked the sun, so the region's inhabitants—an apocryphal people—led the entirety of their lives in unlit days. Iskandar was told that in this remote place he would find a magical spring. If he drank from the spring, he would remain forever young. Its discovery was important to the conqueror. Oracles, seers, omen-readers, dream-interpreters, prophets, and storytellers all warned him that his life was half unspooled. In a few years, they said, he would be resolutely, irrevocably dead.

Everything grew dimmer near the Land of Darkness. The army moved more slowly than usual, dragging tanks of lamp oil and whale fat. After making camp one night, the soldiers woke to discover that they were beyond the reach of any morning. Fires stayed lit, torches were distributed among the men, brass lamps floated between the tents of the nobles. Iskandar asked Aristotle how best to go about the search for the magic spring. Inch by inch, the sage said, and on all fours.

For weeks, Iskandar's army crawled over the earth. For the sake of efficiency, they split up into separate groups. Iskandar looked out from his camp to another in the distance, speckled by the small lights of soldiers drifting to and fro. It was like watching faraway fishing boats from the shore. Iskandar preferred to remain inside his tent and the certainty of its lamps. Nobody, not even the conqueror, could expect how tiring it was to see the world always wavering in flame.

The soldiers found nothing, just blank earth and rock. On occasion, a man stumbled on a damp patch on the ground and he would press his face to it in excitement, only to discover that it was a puddle of piss left by another soldier. They all felt quite small in the vast darkness. Imaginary shapes gathered beyond the circles of light, all hard and serpentine, scaled and clawed, swarming on the verge of attack. The soldiers shivered. Instead of looking for the magical spring they strained their eyes in the shadows, searching for the forms of their doom.

Aristotle reported to Iskandar that the provisions of oil and firewood were running low. If they stayed in this land much longer, it would swallow them. Age is just a number, Aristotle said, and like words, numbers can be made to mean what we want them to mean. Iskandar sighed, accepting that this quest would fail. If indeed I am to die, let it be under the sun.

He ordered an end to the search. Like a saintly procession, his army vacated the Land of Darkness. When they reached its border, they saw morning flicker blue to the west. Soon, real sunlight fell upon them. The men were surprised by each other's faces, the clambering fuzz of their beards, the sharp-ridged cheeks, the round, pale eyes. It seemed impossible that they themselves had these parts.

One soldier missed the retreat. Drunk, he lurched into the dark and collapsed. When he woke, the army had gone. Oh shit, he thought. His torch had blinked out. Scrambling around, he felt a dampness on the ground. His fingers tore into the mud, digging deeper until he reached the oozing, pumping spring. Reason demanded that he restrain himself, but his hangover pushed him to drink. He cupped water into his hands. It tasted sulfurous and vindictive. If this water was the water of life, then not only would he be lost in the Land of Darkness with no way out, he'd be lost there forever. No, the soldier thought, no no no no.

He removed a little dried fish from his pack and lowered his cupped hands into the water. For a few moments, he could feel the dried fish limply floating in his hands. Then, with a wriggle of its salted tail, it leapt out of his grasp.

9. THE ENEMY BENEATH

At last, Iskandar won the war against the fairies. He reclaimed for mankind the four cities they had stolen. The fairies were driven into the sea or enslaved to do human work. Even the fairy queen Araqit found herself enrolled in Iskandar's harem, where the concubines made jokes about her hairy legs.

Many people had lived in the four cities before the fairies took them. Iskandar invited those residents back. Refugees poured in from all over the world, amazed that fate had allowed them something rarely felt: the joy at the end of exile.

Gingerly, they entered their old homes. For many of the returnees, it was hard to tell what, if anything, had changed since they left. A weaver walked between the looms of his workshop, enshrouded in cobwebs. Old thread still hung fixed to the machines. A teenager found the toys on her moth-eaten bed arranged in the exact formation she'd left them as a toddler. A baker opened his ovens and extracted a calcified cake from a veil of dust. In the libraries, none of the books had been unwound from their scrolls. Apparently, the monsters did not care to read.

The absence of any trace of foreign occupation was distressing. It was hard to imagine that gnolls and pimply ogres could lumber about these homes, trade magic goods in the bazaars, or race horses through the squares without leaving some imprint of themselves, some sign that once upon a time a horned hobgoblin undid his stinking boots here and stretched out to snore. If not, what was the point? Why drive us out, why take our homes and our cities if you had no need for them in the first place? Perhaps these creatures had a way of being wholly separate from the observable plane of human life. They could sleep in beds and eat from plates without touching anything at all. But in that case, why bother waging war on humans who until death exist only in the here and now? It was unconscionable. The returnees were appalled by the idea that they had gone into long exile only to have their houses remain empty and their towns entirely unused.

Over time, the fairy past surfaced in different ways in each of the four cities. The first city was on the sea, where all magical creatures come from, and so it had always harbored a kind of intimacy with the other world. Its people knew that a sudden squall was the work of vicious spirits, that every beached whale was driven to sadness by nymphs. In the market, though, the returnees began to notice inexplicable events in their affairs. A vegetable seller would pile twenty ears of corn in her stand only to discover that she had forty instead. Coins of dubious value would, on second glance, be appraised as pure silver. A merchant unraveled a bolt of cloth and found that it was many times as long as he'd imagined. The silk spilled from his table out the door and into the street. Anywhere else in the world, people would celebrate this unexpected wealth. The returnees couldn't help but feel uneasy nor shake the sense that they had received blessings meant for others.

In the second city, people began seeing reflections of monsters in their mirrors. Frenzy gripped the populace. Mobs tore through the street of the mirror makers and made a pogrom of glass. For a whole day, the city was filled with the sound of mirrors and windows being shattered.

The returnees in the third city started dreaming the insensible dreams of fairies. Wives and husbands would shake each other awake, checking each other's faces and private parts. Children slumped into their parents' bedrooms and babbled in magical words. Cats barked in their sleep. Everyone trembled at the approach of dusk. But while the returnees feared the possession of the night, they found that their sleeps during the day were untroubled. So the city flipped its habits and became nocturnal. Only the night watchmen resented this change.

In the fourth city, the returnees wanted to build a temple to Iskandar, the liberator and conqueror, the man-god who restored them to their homes. Architects laid out a plan for a soaring structure. Their temple would need a solid base. At the selected site, they demolished the existing buildings and dug up the grounds. Out came the guts of the city, the old drainage pipes, the foundation stones inscribed in barely readable script. They dug even deeper and were startled to find more strata of human life, a layer of ash on top of a layer of waste on top of the ruins of a stone building, strewn with shards of pottery. The city marveled at the excavation of this forgotten era. See how timeless we are, the citizens said, see how we have endured! Digging a little further, they unearthed bones, lifted with reverence out of the mud. Look, the bodies of our ancestors!

On closer inspection, it became clear that the bones were not human, but belonged to a bestiary of other beings. There were the delicate rib cages of elves, the heavy foreheads of ogres, the long toes of water nymphs. The city rested on the remains of other peoples.

The returnees did not know what to do with this strange testimony. Some citizens insisted that the bones be reburied with due ceremony, unless the city wanted to upset the spirits of the fairies and incite further conflict. Others thought the bones should be thrown away, forgotten and expunged. In the end, the merchants won. The remains found their way into the markets, as jewelry or powders for virility or curious relics. They were treasured and then forgotten over the years, rediscovered as signs not of another world, but of another time. Poking about his father's study on a weekend afternoon, a boy lifted a skeletal elf hand from the cabinet and wondered how different it was from his own.

10. A SPELL ON THE CONQUEROR'S PENIS

Like many other fathers, the king of Kashmir was rather upset at having to hand over his daughter to Iskandar. He stayed up all night, a knot of misery in his chest. Iskandar's army sat encamped outside the king's walls. Somewhere in that labyrinth of rope and canvas, his daughter could be in bed with the invaders. The king of Kashmir raged. Only poor men and ambitious ministers release their girls to a harem.

A local holy man came to comfort the king. I will make it such that when Iskandar tries to have your daughter, he will not be able to pierce the clouds. Pierce the clouds? the king blinked. I mean, to distend himself. Distend himself? To perform, he will not be able to perform. The king nodded, and the holy man went away to cast his spells.

That night, when Iskandar visited his new acquisition, he was flaccid. This is strange, he thought, I've barely drunk anything. He apologized to the princess of Kashmir. He was no harder when he tried the next night, nor the night after that. What is wrong with me? he beseeched his advisors. Have you tried to rouse yourself with other women? Aristotle asked. Of course, and it's all working as it's meant to, I assure you. But with the princess of Kashmir? With the princess of Kashmir, nothing, a dried-up spout. Odd . . . she is quite lovely. Iskandar leaned his head against a pole of the tent. I know she is, he said, I've never met anybody so gorgeous . . . her face is like the moon that poets see on the necks of beautiful women.

Aristotle comforted Iskandar. Reason leads me to conclude that there's only one possible source for your incapacity: a magical spell. A spell? Yes, a spell cast on behalf of the king. How can we get the spell lifted? I don't know how this foreign magic works, Aristotle admitted, but the most reliable method tends to be this: find the holy man who cast the spell, and kill him.

Iskandar's agents spread through Kashmir and rounded up all the holy men. They were tortured and interrogated. None confessed to casting the spell, nor even having the ability to do so. So they were tortured some more. Taking his captors aside, one holy man pointed to a rival and said, It's him, I swear to you, it's him . . . execute him and let the rest of us innocents go. Both informant and the informed upon were killed, but when Iskandar with great expectation went to the princess of Kashmir, he found himself no abler than before.

Kill all the holy men, he yelled at Aristotle, slit their throats, break their fingers, squish their toes. That wouldn't be the wisest thing to do. Yes, yes, yes, kill them. It's taken a lot of work to subdue this kingdom, we don't want the people of Kashmir to rise up against us. To hell with the people of Kashmir, what about my penis?

Aristotle looked at him as if he were a child. The sage cleared his throat very loudly and then said nothing at all.

The conqueror relented. The holy men were released after they vowed that from this day on they would never cast spells on Iskandar. He accepted that his desire for the princess of Kashmir would not be fulfilled. His advisors asked him to let her go.

She won't be of much use to you, Aristotle said, you may as well restore her to her family. No, Iskandar said, I'll keep her. Why? Every once in a while, you'll bring her to me so I can stare at her face. That's cruel. What can I say, I'm greedy . . . I won't let go of the things I can't have.

II. THE WAQ-WAQ TREE

In Ceylon, the local king suggested Iskandar visit the tomb of Adam. Iskandar went with his entourage and delivered offerings to the tomb's Indian guardians. The Indians told him to climb to the top of the nearby mountain. There was a great wonder at its peak. When he was cast onto earth, Adam landed on the mountain and left an indelible mark. Iskandar lay down in the giant footprint of Adam, fully the length of a grown man.

Adam arrived here, one of the Indians explained, Eve fell near Mecca, Satan in Qum, and the serpent in Esfahan. That makes sense, Iskandar said, Esfahan is full of temptations, but Qum is a pretty wretched place. The Indian guide carried on. Adam was so miserable that he spent years weeping on the mountain, and from his tears all these bitter plants and weeds grew. He pointed to the vegetation on one slope, thick with brambles and leaves laced purple. But then, as it is written in the Quran, God forgave Adam and accepted him into His love, and for years Adam wept tears of joy for being allowed back into the fold . . . from these tears sprung fragrant and wholesome plants. He showed Iskandar the other side of the mountain, which was stripped bare save for the occasional bright green bush. Seems pretty barren to me, the conqueror said. The Indian smiled apologetically. That's the side we harvest for tea.

Iskandar desperately wanted to see the waq-waq tree, another wonder of this part of the world. Does it exist? he asked the Indian. Is it true what they say about the talking tree? That instead of fruit, the tree flowers human heads that can speak? That some trees even sprout full human bodies, and the natives, whenever they please, go to the tree and have sex with its fruit? Maybe even your mother was the fruit of a waq-waq tree?

The Indian led Iskandar to one of these trees. It was the tallest he had ever seen. Long green fronds bent in a dome from its slender trunk. There was a cluster of shaggy brown heads at the top. They shifted in the breeze and murmured, though Iskandar could only hear their words vaguely. What are they saying? he asked. One of them wants to meet you, the Indian said. Do I need to climb the tree? No, the head will descend on its own. There was a reluctant snapping noise. Here it comes, the Indian said.

In horror, Iskandar watched as one of the heads tumbled down, knocking the trunk of the tree again and again as it fell. It smashed at his feet, a speechless mess of white pulp and husk. The Indian crouched and sifted its remains. Bad luck, he said, most of the time they're more eloquent.

12. THE WALL OF YAJUJ AND MAJUJ

Deep into the sixth clime of the earth, Iskandar came upon a poor and haggard people. They welcomed him and his entourage with bland stew and millet beer. No country had ever seemed so foreign to Iskandar. In the damp, smoky hall, he struggled to understand what their leader was saying. Is this man even speaking in words, Aristotle? The sage lowered his chin to concentrate. You know, Aristotle said after some time listening, it really is hard to tell.

Through a process of gestures and broken speech, Iskandar learned that he had now reached the end. Beyond this province were only wasteland and the ocean that bounded everything. Well, that's good to know, Iskandar said, nothing to conquer over that way. The leader of the remote people asked if Iskandar's army would stay some time. I'm Iskandar, Iskandar said, of the bloodline of the shahs of Persia, heir to the kings of Macedonia, son of an Egyptian god . . . I stay and I go as I please. Oh excellent, the leader communicated, that's great, please stay as long as you like.

Iskandar was surprised. Most people are more precious about their sovereignty, he said. We'll give it to you freely, without a fight, with regular tribute. Really? Iskandar turned to Aristotle, who shrugged. Yes, but on one condition . . . you build us a wall. The man mimed with both hands the shape of a wall. A wall? Yes, a wall to block the demons.

The next day, the leader showed Iskandar and his entourage what he wanted. He brought them to a narrow pass at the head of a valley. Through the pass, he gestured, is the land of Yajuj and Majuj. Yajuj and Majuj? Iskandar asked. Harbingers of apocalypse, Aristotle whispered, ferocious demons, bringers of end times, that kind of thing. The leader continued. Evil spirits come from over there . . . they terrorize our dreams, we hear them scratching at our doors at night, sometimes they even kidnap our children. I don't see anything, Iskandar said. There seemed to be little difference between the lands on either side of the valley. Please, the leader insisted, a wall blocking this pass would protect the entire world. Unconvinced, Iskandar turned to his advisors. These people are crazy . . . what's the point of building a wall here?

Aristotle pulled Iskandar aside. Sometimes things are built to serve a function, the sage said, and sometimes they are built just to be built. So you think we should do this. Paper molders, poems get distorted from one generation to the next . . . a monument in stone, however, lasts many, many lifetimes. Building a wall will project me into the future, will it? Yes, of course . . . and if it delays the coming of Yajuj and Majuj and the end of the world, well, then nobody could accuse you of vanity.

Using the talents of his army's metallurgists, bricklayers, engineers, and sappers, Iskandar raised a wall at the neck of the pass. It took some time and much effort, but like the best conquerors, he had a lot of men. The work never stopped. Each stone had to be cut to fit the next, since too much mortar in a defensive wall made its collapse more likely. All the iron bolts that joined the stones had to be coated in molten lead. If they weren't, exposed iron would rust, then the bolts fray, the stones gradually slip out of joint, and soon, invisible from the outside, cracks would spread like spiderwebs within the edifice. An inscription was carved above the false gate: I, Iskandar, raised this barrier to protect the people of the world until the world ends and this barrier falls. Copper sheathed the parapets so that they glowed in the mornings and smoldered at dusk.

Every once in a while during the construction, Iskandar would climb the scaffolds and stare over the lip of the wall. The ocean spread gray to the horizon. Scrub fell down the side of the hills to a threadbare quilt of rowan. After the heather, only sand and emptiness. Nothing moved on that side. He stayed up on the wall one night, peering into the dark, vainly hoping to hear some peculiar movement, some indication that the forces of Yajuj and Majuj resented his great masonry. He left disappointed.

Aristotle added several ingenious devices to the wall. Since Iskandar had no intention of stationing any soldiers there, the sage designed mechanisms that repetitively beat metal drums. The hammering gave the impression that the wall was in a constant state of activity, always being built and improved. Aristotle also positioned a number of clever trumpets on the ramparts. They sounded when the wind blew through them at the right angle. Without a soul defending it, the wall brimmed with defiant noise.

Over time, of course, these contraptions failed. The hammers slowed and stopped beating altogether. Owls nested in the open mouths of the trumpets, blocking the old brass tubes with their feathers. No clarion call came from the horns—only the occasional squawk. Silence reigned along the wall, with one exception. If travelers came up to that monumental edifice and pressed ears to its stone, they would hear distantly from the other side the furious, indefatigable sound of scratching.

13. KANIFU UNDRESSED

Iskandar returned to China and defeated its khan in battle. It was a close-run thing. For much of the day, his soldiers were beaten back by the khan's champion, who toppled cavalcades of *sipahis* and splintered the advance of the phalanx. Eventually, the champion was subdued. Iskandar himself flung a lasso around the warrior's neck and dragged him back to camp.

The victory celebration went on late into the night. Like all good kings, Iskandar drank goblet after goblet of wine. His noble warriors tried to outdo one another in recounting their feats on the battlefield. Each boastful tally won rewards from Iskandar: a sum of gold, a jewel, a bracelet, a slave, a parcel of newly conquered land. Once this redistribution was complete, Iskandar and his nobles searched for further entertainment. Nobody had any interest in the bards because the battle still surged fresh in the mind. Nobody could watch acrobats roll around because their japes mocked the energy of war. Instead, the men demanded that the Chinese champion be brought from his cage.

Iskandar asked him what he was called. My name is Kanifu, the champion said. Long hair fell across red cheeks. His plate armor seethed in the firelight. Iskandar praised his valor on the battlefield. My army always has room for good men, the conqueror said; indeed some of my best servants—he waved in the direction of the drunk nobles—surrendered their service to me in war . . . Why not join me? Kanifu said nothing and didn't raise his eyes. Submit to me, the conqueror said, and you will see that the world is far greater than your dusty China.

Kanifu stayed silent. Look at me, Iskandar said, you may look at me. The champion remained motionless. The nobles began to grumble. What ingratitude. Your wretched life has been spared, and you won't give the conqueror the generosity of your eyes. Put the bastard in his place. Humiliate him. Iskandar lifted his hand. Strip this Kanifu, he commanded.

It took some time to undo all the ties and buckles. Two men had to battle with the seams of the armor. Kanifu did not resist. While he was undressed, he lifted his head and looked at the smoky sky. Iskandar studied the rolling turn of the man's chin, the tundra of sideburns, the soft jaw. You are exceptionally young, he said, younger even than I was when I first went about killing.

They undid the gauntlets first. Kanifu's knuckles were pinched and blue. Then off came the rerebrace and the vambrace. He had slender arms. The pauldrons were made of such heavy metal that Iskandar's servants had to let them thud to the earth. Kanifu's shoulders were narrow and Iskandar marveled at the slightness of the warrior who had cut down so many of his own. Each pin in the gorget had to be pried loose before the entire piece could be removed, baring a pale and heaving neck. Off came the cuisses and poleyns, sabatons and greaves. Kanifu's shins were hairless. The champion closed his eyes as they took off the plackart and fauld. Finally, they lifted off the breastplate, dented by so many blows.

Kanifu stood in the filthy linen shift he wore beneath his armor. It was so soaked in blood and sweat that it clung to his skin. The nobles could see his shape, the unambiguous swelling of breasts, the sullen hips. They fell silent. Chinese men have strange bodies, one noble whispered to another. This man, the other said, is a woman.

Cover her up, Iskandar said, and take her to my pavilion. They all watched in silence as a shawl was draped around Kanifu and she was led away. Iskandar concentrated on his wine while the nobles resumed their conversations, but they were no longer merry. One by one, his men made their excuses and returned to their tents.

By the time Iskandar came to his own tent, his attendants had washed Kanifu and dressed her in a silk shift. They rubbed ointments on her skin, perfume on her neck and wrists, brushed her hair to a dark shimmer, tucked a flower behind one ear. They made her recline on a couch with a platter of melon and cups of wine and await the arrival of the conqueror. Her hands were chained.

My valiant lady, Iskandar said, forgive the way you were treated . . . you must think me a brutish warlord, but I assure you I'm as courtly as a prince. He drank from his cup. In a fold of the tent, a musician strummed a quiet tune. Why have your people dressed me like this? Kanifu asked. You have such exquisite eyebrows, Iskandar said, your eyes are shaped like dreams. I will not be your slave. The hour is too late for harsh words . . . Tell me, do you enjoy poetry? I'm a soldier, you will not touch me. Hush, and listen to verse.

"I chained my heart to your locks," Iskandar recited, reaching out to her. "If it's not for slavery, free it. Shake out the dust on your head." Imprison me in iron, Kanifu said, not silk. "One drunk on you needs no wine." My people will be avenged. "Yearning for you, no trace of me remains." She wrestled away from Iskandar, who pursued her around the tent. The musician continued to play. You will never have me, Kanifu said. Yes, I will. Iskandar pinned her to the floor and brought his face very close to hers. Kanifu jerked her body like a fish in the air and struck him in the mouth. He looked at her in shock, feeling the blood rush to his lips. "The world burns caught in your gaze," he said.

14. THE SUBMERSIBLE

With the known world conquered and his enemies subdued, Iskandar set his sights on the sea. But my lord, his advisors said, your navies already control the ocean . . . your ships are anchored in every port. Yes, we already have the surface of the seas, Iskandar said, but I want to go underneath. He sketched a design for his craftsmen. They startled at the plans and leaked them to Aristotle. The sage interrupted Iskandar's breakfast. You can't be serious, Aristotle said, you can't actually intend to do this. Where's your spirit of adventure, Iskandar replied, where's your curiosity? You're going to drown. Nonsense. Everybody else will drown trying to rescue you. If any of my subjects are trustworthy, it's the glass-blowers . . . they won't let me down. Have some pity, Aristotle said, can you imagine me, at my age, lifting up my robes and diving in after you?

The craftsmen followed Iskandar's instructions. When the contraption was ready, he presented it to all his advisors and nobles. They muttered around the oblong object. Iskandar's wives and concubines watched from behind filigreed screens. In this submersible, he explained, I will journey to the bottom of the sea. The submersible was shaped like a bell, narrower above, wider at its base. It was made of glass, in places reinforced with bronze, with cables flowing from the top like the dreadlocks of a mystic. The various names of god spiraled in enamel around its belly. We will push out into the ocean, Iskandar said, I will climb into the submersible and then you will lower it into the water. His advisors were horrified. Suppose something goes wrong, they said, suppose you need help? Oh don't worry, Iskandar said, if I need help, I'll just pull one of those ropes and you'll hear, on the ship, the ringing of many bells. The court shuffled skeptically, so he felt compelled to demonstrate how the submersible would work. He popped open the hatch, slid inside, and sealed himself in. See, he knocked against the glass, it's solid . . . nothing will happen to me. He continued to rap the glass to prove its strength. For once, his advisors and women couldn't hear a thing he said.

Many boats accompanied Iskandar's expedition out of the harbor and into the deeper waters of the bay. On deck, priests of various faiths gave him their blessings. He entered the submersible and signaled for it to be lowered. Half sunk in the water, it stopped. Iskandar looked up to see why. We're just checking the rope ties one more time, Aristotle yelled. None of the words could penetrate the diving bell. Iskandar searched the expressions of his men, peering down over the prow of the ship. Their faces were smudged through the shaped glass, their mouths and noses growing fat and small, their white teeth giant, so it seemed that they were in turns ecstatic and glum. Everything was hazy above the line of the water, while the world beneath burbled into dark focus. Completing their checks, his men let the bell plunge below.

Iskandar marveled at how underwater, sunlight seemed to shatter in fragments across the surface. Fish darted under his feet. He never expected the water to be so green, for the ragged sun to slice through in beams. The sight reminded him of his childhood when, as a pupil imprisoned in the library, he would watch dust motes drift in and out of the light.

It grew darker the lower he sank. The arc of his vision narrowed. A cloud of stingrays skimmed alongside him, circling for an instant. He pressed his nose to the glass and watched them beat their wings and swim away—Like great pillows of flatbread plucked from the tandoor, he thought, I must remember to describe them to the illuminators. He spoke aloud and the words echoed within the diving bell. It occurred to him then that he was alone, and that he could not remember the last time he had been so alone. There was always somebody nearby, a servant, an advisor, a woman, pairs of ears and eyes to affirm the things he said and did.

The submersible kept falling. This far down, the sun above was more distinct and restricted in its effect. Iskandar could just about see the barnacled shadows of his ships and the lines of their anchors. So many people choose solitude, Iskandar thought, hermits, wanderers, saints . . . if they can endure it for years, surely I can handle it for just a little while. Seaweed smoked to the surface in tendrils. An eel snapped against the glass and looked Iskandar in the eye.

There were thousands of stories about the mysteries of the ocean, of the cities mermen built from coral, islands sprouting from the back hair of leviathans, the treasure of King Solomon's shipwrecks. Iskandar hoped for the grace of a fleet of turtles. But as he dropped further down, the immensity of the sea resolved around him. The murk conjured little interruptions of life—a group of jellyfish unfurled like the caps of mushrooms—that only reminded Iskandar of the small range of his wonder. I will have to do this many, many more times, he thought, just to feel that I've done it at all.

The submersible hit the bottom, rolling a bit so that Iskandar pitched from side to side. It came to a rest on the edge of a ridge. Enough sunlight reached here. He had always imagined the sea floor to be a flat plain, as even and endless as the ocean itself. Instead, he looked out on complicated topography, seaweed forests clambering up a hill, rivers of coral pouring through the neck of a valley. Porcelain crabs strolled along the glass. A harem of bluehead wrasse poked out of their coral apartments before disappearing back indoors. Clownfish nuzzled the fronds of an anemone.

At a slightly lower elevation, at the far end of what was visible to him, he saw lines protruding from the floor. There was something suspiciously human in those shapes, the curve of a hull, the splintering of a mast. He decided to get closer. Iskandar pushed against one side of the submersible. It fell, dropping off the tiny cliff, smashing coral and raising a mist of sand. Iskandar rolled over and over.

When the submersible stopped rolling, Iskandar found himself separated only by the glass from the moldering remains of a whale. Dizzy, he lifted himself to his knees. Starfish sprawled in the whale's empty eye socket. The creature was so large that parts of it were in different stages of decomposition. Lampreys sucked on the flesh of its haunches. Its flippers had crumbled away, revealing long fingering bones that dug into the ground. Sea creatures of every shape and texture, worms and mollusks, fish and eels, crowded like refugees in the whale's caverns. All that survived of its mouth were ranks of pointed teeth and the pale cudgel of a jaw.

Pity overwhelmed Iskandar. It pained him to see such a grand being reduced this way, denied the privacy of death, becoming home to a ghoulish society of scroungers. Iskandar swayed. His dull image appeared in the glass, refracted in the irregular turns and bubbles, so that a million visions of his face ghosted in front of him. We have to save this whale, he thought, it deserves a better memorial than this. He pulled the rope that rung the alarm up above.

Soon, his men reeled in the submersible. Iskandar watched the rotting edifice of the whale recede, felt the submersible rotate as it spun up to the light, teetering in a rain of marine snow, each vegetal flake glowing. When the diving bell breached the surface, Iskandar hid his eyes from the sun. His men levered the submersible on board and popped him free.

I have to go back down, he said once he had recovered his breath. Don't be foolish, Aristotle said, that's enough heroism for the day. I found something . . . a shipwreck of sorts, and I want it brought to the surface. Why? Iskandar grabbed Aristotle's hand. Because greatness doesn't deserve this ignominy of the sea. Fine, but you're in no shape to go yourself. I suppose not, Iskandar conceded, send an engineer to see how it can be done.

An engineer was placed in the submersible. He was told to estimate the length of rope needed to secure the corpse. The vessel was winched overboard. Iskandar prayed for the engineer as he disappeared below the water. Only minutes later, the bells rang and the cables shivered. Bring him back up, Aristotle yelled. The men heaved and pulled. Eventually, the diving bell returned to the surface. It had broken cleanly at the middle. Its other half, including its passenger, had fallen away. Iskandar lay down in his cabin. He imagined the poor engineer sinking to the bottom, lying forever folded in the whale.

THE FALL OF AN EYELASH

Forough left her country when she was still a college student. Her family smuggled her away at night without letting her tell any friends. She kissed her young brother, tucked him into bed, and watched him fall asleep like it was any other night before a morning of tooth-brushing and tea. Her parents sent her over the desert with jewelry sewed into the linings of her clothes. She carried a silk carpet so fine you could fold it to the size of a bib. It alone paid for much of her journey. The smugglers admired her carpet, turning it back and forth in the light and praising its deft weave, as if they could sell rugs as easily as they hurtled people into new lives.

After crossing many borders, she arrived at her refuge. The country that took her in was green and made from clean lines. Most people were kind to Forough, but kindness is sometimes easier to give than to receive. They found the story of her voyage so courageous that they insisted she tell it over and over again. This exhausted her and offered further proof, as if she needed it, that while an exile can escape her country, she can never escape her exile.

It didn't help that her work made her think at all times of her homeland. She studied and then taught the medieval poetry of her country. There was something unsettling in the sight of a blonde student reciting with perfect meter and inflection a seven-hundred-year-old verse in her language. But why should I be unnerved, she thought, this poetry of love is not just for my people . . . it's for everybody.

Lonely, she allowed herself to love men in her new country. Several filled her years in college and then graduate school. Thanks to them, she broadened the range of the freedoms and sufferings of her solitary life. She eventually settled on Jonas. He was slightly balding and had thin lips, but he loved her deeply. He cooked, buzzed about her with jokes and curiosities, and didn't make her miss her family any more than she already did.

Her family blessed the wedding from afar. It was dangerous for them to speak to her, so messages had to be sent indirectly. Through an acquaintance in a nearby town—a distant relative, really—she learned that her parents and brother had feasted in her honor. For his part, her relative brought the newlyweds an enormous box of kebabs and rice. They ate and toasted the future with schnapps. When her relative left, she refused to open the windows for days, letting the smell of the meat linger.

As both a refugee and a wife, Forough learned new customs. One of them had to do with wishes. Every time Jonas spotted a stray eyelash on her face, he would rush to place it on the tip of a finger. A wish, he'd say, any wish. Then he'd make her blow it off. If for whatever reason she failed—sometimes still damp after a shower, the rogue eyelash clung more desperately to the skin—he would laugh and make her keep blowing until the eyelash vanished. See, it's gone . . . the fates will never deny you, he'd promise her.

Forough, who was a quick study, didn't believe him. A resilient eyelash was as good as a curse, or whatever was the opposite of a wish. She dreaded those moments when he'd make her wish on an eyelash. There was, after all, only one wish inside her, one overwhelming desire whose fulfillment seemed so improbable that it could hardly rest on an eyelash. Her family remained far away, her country was still closed to her. She saw no prospect of reunion and no reason for its hope. Why mock the unbridgeable distance between her and them? And why drain, with every unanswered wish, what little magic there was in the fall of an eyelash?

So she began wishing for small things. A good breakfast. Students who did their reading. An orgasm. Occasionally, she wished for a victory for Djurgårdens, Jonas's favorite football team. More often than not, these little wishes came true. Jonas would come home on a Saturday, red-cheeked and burping from the beer, and spin her around in triumph. Be grateful, she'd say to him, my eyelash scored your goals.

One day in the shower together, Jonas found an eyelash that had slid into the lee of her nose. Make a wish, he said. Forough held him close and contemplated the eyelash on his outstretched finger. No obvious wish came to her. In this sedate country she was becoming increasingly sedate herself, untroubled by life's little infelicities. Djurgårdens had won its games this season, sex with Jonas was pleasing, her students were sharper than she expected. She cleared her head. I wish to see my brother soon, she thought. She blew with the force of a thousand wishes. The eyelash, though still damp, disappeared from Jonas's finger.

The next day the house phone rang. It was her relative. Peace be upon you, he said. And you, she replied. Your parents transmitted a message through my family, he told her, they feared it would be intercepted otherwise. This is what it says:

We are sending your brother over the desert route . . . He'll cross the border by the end of the week and then make his way to you . . . God bless you both.

Forough was so shaken that she offered her relative a cup of tea, as if he were standing right in front of her.

Jonas helped set up consultations with asylum seekers' networks and a meeting with government officials. They assured Forough that once her brother arrived, his application for asylum would be expedited. He would receive the same benefits she had received. Her new country would become his, too.

The furniture in their living room had to be rearranged. She bought a sofa bed, ingenious little storage units disguised as footstools, a small TV so that he could watch what he pleased, like he was used to at home. Jonas left a Djurgårdens scarf folded on the sofa, ready for her brother's arrival. Unable to sleep at night, Forough sat in the dim living room longing for her brother to fill it with his snores. She remembered the loneliness of the desert crossing, the menacing moon. She imagined him bundled in the back of a jeep, watching the dunes slouch away.

In the shower the next morning, she pulled Jonas's face close. Her fingers searched its every bump and slope. But she was disappointed. After drying her hair and putting it up, she turned to him. Do you see one? she asked. See what? An eyelash, do you see a stray eyelash? Jonas moved her face in and out of the light and shook his head.

Forough's quest for an eyelash consumed her. In between classes, she'd stand before the mirror in the washroom for minutes, alternately looking up close and at a distance. No fallen eyelash revealed itself. She thought she found one—spotting a hair on the crest of the cheekbone—only to realize that it was too thick and blunt. It had descended from an eyebrow. She pondered for a moment the metaphysical qualities of brow hairs, those shingles of the eye, and decided that they would not do as substitutes. When being gracious, people in her country would sometimes say, Please, walk on my eyelashes. Nobody ever invited you to walk on their eyebrows.

Jonas understood the urgency of her search, obliging her with frequent scans that yielded nothing. His own face offered few wishes. Now more than ever, Forough resented the stubbornness of his eyelashes, which were short and fair to the point of being invisible, with none of her dark abundance. He was sorry for their austerity, blinking over and over again in attempts to make an eyelash drop.

With no lash falling from their eyelids, Forough remembered all the times she had blown an eyelash away indifferently. She had grown accustomed to making little wishes casually, without thinking: wishes for a cloudless sky, for ripe tomatoes, for a worthy councilor to win a local election, for publication in an academic journal, for the mastery of foreign languages, for a glimpse of the northern lights, for flatbread and cheese and mint and walnuts. What a waste, she thought. Her brother was about to reach the border. The breadth of a single vanished eyelash might be enough to push him across. But when she needed it most, her eyes refused to surrender a single wish.

The night before her brother was due to cross, Jonas volunteered to pull out one of her eyelashes. She gasped. Are you crazy? What kind of idea is that? He shrugged optimistically. An eyelash is an eyelash, no? She shook her head and smiled. Only if the eyelash fell on its own upon the cheek would it have any power. To force a wish would be to violate the natural order of wishes. They laughed at themselves and Jonas held her against his chest, kissing the top of her head. He felt an unspeakable guilt for bringing his wife into a tradition that might betray her.

Without waking her husband, Forough climbed out of bed in the middle of the night and went to the bathroom. She found a pair of tweezers and brought them close to her eyes. The steel hovered over her vision like a fighter jet. She thought of her brother alone on his journey, clutching all his papers to his chest, the letters and documents and proofs of being that at once imprisoned him and promised him a future with her. The tweezers pinched down and an eyelash soon lay on her palm. She blew it away.

A few days later, her relative rang. The smugglers had delivered her brother successfully across the border, but he'd disappeared since. An intermediary had been missed, a hostel not checked into, a flight skipped. Somewhere along the shadowy paths of his journey into exile, her brother had fallen away. Where is he? she asked in desperation. Does anybody know how to find him? Is he alive? Her relative had no answers. He promised to make what inquiries he could and to be in touch with any updates as he received them.

She sobbed, something she had rarely done in her life. Jonas came to comfort her, but she pushed him away. The tears spilled down her face. She tried to distract herself from her misery by thinking of the heroines of the poetry of her homeland, those willowy princesses bursting with such epic sadness that they could turn a desert to mud with their tears. If she could, she would flood the world and drown the injustice of its borders. When she was calmer she went to the bathroom to clean herself up. There on her face, glistening in the dry bed of her anguish, was a single eyelash.

LETTERS HOME

I

The pharaoh Necko was not content to rule the Upper and the Lower. He wanted knowledge of the whole. So he plopped a crew of Phoenicians down in the Red Sea and told them to go home the long way. Off they went south, pulling on oars and cursing with lemon breath their bad luck for being alive in the time of the Egyptians.

The edges of an entire continent watched the tentacle creep of Phoenician oars. On board, the Phoenicians didn't see Africa as Africa. They had no sense of its contiguity. At the Cape of Good Hope, they thought they had crested the world. Mount Cameroon belched the fiery promise of its ending. The Gambia River spread wide as a sea. Finally rounding Bojador after several attempts, the Phoenicians welcomed the green of the northern ocean. They relished its cold tirades. If man was made for land, the Phoenicians were made for wind.

For much of their journey, they were puzzled to find the sun hovering on their right side. We would say now, reasonably, that this was the effect of crossing hemispheres, of leaving the north for the south. But they did not have this illusory sense of up and down. The world hadn't been distorted into place by maps. Instead, they followed the unbroken line of coast, willing it like sunrise to arc into the circle of their longing.

Every few months, they stopped for a while. They found a

nameless harbor, beached their boat, scraped the hull clean, undid all the rigging, patched the lonely sail. They stretched out to sleep in little cotton camps. If, by chance, they met with locals, it was quick and rough. The Phoenicians left little behind, certainly not their names. Sometimes, when searching for traces of the vanished foreigners, locals would come across inexplicable plots of alfalfa, growing wild and alien.

Eventually, the Phoenicians skimmed past the Pillars of Hercules into the Mediterranean. The crew was chapped and blackened, dressed in new clothes, furnished with new slaves, drunk on gourds of palm liquor. When they pulled into the harbor at the mouth of the Nile, the Egyptians gathered to marvel at their menagerie of captured animals.

The Phoenicians asked to see the pharaoh Necko and collect their reward. Too bad, they were told, he died years ago. The new pharaoh had no interest in their travels. In fact, he had no interest in reminding people of the old pharaoh. He seized the Phoenicians' boat and confiscated their exotic animals and slaves.

Some of the sailors made it home to Phoenicia. Few people remembered them. They were looked at as ghosts or as strangers, which would have been harder to bear if they didn't feel it themselves.

2

For a few centuries, many people wanted to believe that a medieval Welsh prince sailed to America, discovering the continent long before Columbus. They dated his voyage to 1170. They had minimal proof. There was no real documentary evidence for the expedition of Prince Madoc, only an accumulation of folklore passed down through the British aristocracy. Nor was there any archaeological evidence of a Welsh colony in the Americas, though much time was spent scouring the midlands for traces.

The believers of this theory studied every axhead and arrowhead, rampart and earthwork, for a suggestion of mist-wreathed Wales. If those hard things offered any clues, it was only in thin and reedy whispers. So fantastic rumors spread: in Alabama, breastplates emblazoned with a Welsh coat of arms; a stone citadel in Kentucky; old Welsh landings in Mexico, Florida, and Newfoundland; and, most of all, clear-eyed Indians across the continent who spoke Welsh.

Several men in the seventeenth century claimed separately to have been saved by knowledge of Welsh. Captured by surly Indian tribesmen, they squealed for mercy in their mother tongue. The Indians muttered among themselves and then circled around the captives. They smiled and produced meandering sounds that resembled Welsh. The Welshmen were freed; their comrades who spoke no Welsh were killed.

Thomas Jefferson asked Meriwether Lewis to look out for Indians who spoke Welsh. Brigham Young dispatched Welsh-speaking missionaries to various tribes south of Utah in the hope of recovering Madoc's descendants. By the middle of the nineteenth century, the consensus was that the Mandan people of the Midwest were the most likely heirs of the Welsh prince. But the population was so decimated by smallpox and displaced by conquest that it was hard to determine if there were any real Mandans left. They had become a myth in their own time.

This was real: Three Hopi men were brought to Salt Lake City in 1863. They were sat down in a room full of Welshmen. For hours, the Welsh speakers flooded them with syllables, fragments, full sentences in all the dialects of the valleys and coasts, in old Welsh, in ancient Brythonic. The Hopi men were strung up in the singsong of Merlin. They cut their way free with the sharpest knife they had. We're very sorry, they said in English, but we don't understand a word.

3

Many vessels cluttered the heaving floats from West Africa to the Caribbean. There were human bodies, of course, those chained people destined for the sugar plantations, full of despair and anger and other hungry thoughts. But there were also mosquitoes for whom the journey across the ocean must have spanned many generations. The mosquitoes roamed and ate and spawned and died. What is more infinite in the mind of a blood-sucking insect: the slave ship's multitude of bodies, its countless miles of veins and whispering capillaries, or the lonely plots of African wetland that the mosquito once imagined as its own? Perhaps some folkloric memory of the sky persevered among the mosquitoes, transmitted in the dark from mother to larvae. A male mosquito lives only ten to twenty days. The life of a female mosquito can last as long as one hundred days. With favorable winds and a sure navigator, it could have been that an ancient female mosquito emerged from the ship's belly to fizz in the light of another continent.

The mosquitoes brought yellow fever to Haiti. It offered a grisly liberation, sweeping through the ranks of Napoleon's brigades with such relentlessness that as many as half of the French troops were laid low by the fever. Guerrilla warfare, desertion, and a British blockade did in the rest. Haiti was free. The triumphant black armies took the cities of their erstwhile masters. Whites were expelled, their property seized.

But some whites were allowed to stay. Several hundred Poles chose to settle along the sea, building a hamlet whose future name, Cazale, was a Creole estrangement of one of their surnames. History regularly produces these little enclaves of the uncanny. With their usual bad luck, the Poles had lost their own nation several years earlier to Russia and Austria. Napoleon embraced them into his legions and promised to restore their country. But he found the Poles too revolutionary for his liking, so he packed them off to Haiti to reclaim the colony, where he hoped they would do him the favor of dying.

There were Poles who stayed loyal to France, who bellowed and expired on the ramparts of Cap Français or in the mountains, places equally far from Poland. There were Poles who died, like everybody else, of yellow fever. And there were Poles who wondered whether they, the downtrodden of Europe, stolen from their woodlands to do the savagery of others, were blacker than they had realized, and simply switched sides.

When Pope John Paul II visited Haiti in 1983, local leaders and clergy produced various specimens for the pontiff's amusement, men and women fair enough to suggest some plausible history of Polishness. Polish photographers still journey to modern-day Cazale. They search for light skin, for green and blue eyes, blond hair. They shoot freely, wandering through back gardens, claiming any face that isn't in their (and our) view entirely black. A grandmotherly smile beams up from the washing. A square-jawed youth angles his head and looks away while a much darker man trims his hair. A nurse holds up a pale baby to the camera. There is no memory in these photos, only desire.

Look instead at icons of Ezili Dantò, the Haitian spirit of independence, a fiery beauty who supports righteous causes and now blesses the weddings of lesbians, who loves nothing more than Barbancourt rum, fried pork, and cigarettes. Draped in gold, she has three scars on her cheek received during the war against the French. She carries her daughter Anais in the bend of her left arm.

In every aspect of framing and composition, her image copies the Black Madonna of Częstochowa, that famous icon of the Virgin Mary whose lithograph Polish soldiers worshipped in the heat and desolation of Haiti's war. We can imagine the transfer of the image; it snapped as a banner above the Polish regiments, it was worn by many Poles as an amulet. In an act of unexpected friendship and common feeling, a Polish soldier may have gifted his amulet to a Haitian rebel, his black comrade. Or maybe he had his throat slit. The Black Madonna, who could not help him, was plucked from his corpse.

She carried her own military history. Her icon was pierced by the arrows of Tatars and slashed by radical Hussite iconoclasts. The legend goes that she was painted on planks of wood in Constantinople by the apostle Luke. Before that, she was just a cedar table, on whose face Mary herself once ate a meal.

4

An Anglo-Saxon poet walked alone through the remains of a fallen Roman city. His people were responsible for its devastation. Maybe they kept a guilty conscience, because they avoided the ruined town as an evil place haunted by toga-clad wraiths steaming in the baths, spectral fishmongers hurling phosphorescent cod across the plazas. This barbarian, however, was brave enough to enter (poets have absolutely nothing to lose). He gazed in awe at the walls burst long ago, their iron steadings bound with rust. He picked his way between the toppled battlements. Since he only ever knew buildings made from wood and thatch, he was convinced that giants sculpted the enormous stonework.

And yet this world of archways and columns and marble solemnity didn't seem so far off from his own. He paused in a gutted basilica, watching the birds be birds under its cavernous eaves, and could only think of the big gloom of his mead hall, the bearded warriors drunk and asleep on the boards, the women yawning and wringing beer from their skirts. He came into a building that once housed baths, its pools now full of debris, and recalled how he hated bathing, the pink itch of being clean. Lichen and rime had clambered over the towers. Among the broken pillars of a courthouse, he saw the shadows of his own people's justice: his thane weighing the blood price of a crime, the criminal pacing steadfast to his dismemberment. The barbarian felt the border dissolve between his living world and the empty city. The ruin became his own. He was overtaken by this notion: this city of giants may seem so other, but it is the fate of my people. He returned quivering to his damp wooden hamlet, shaken even though he hadn't seen a single ghoul. Nothing—not even his name—survives him except a poem and its record of his ancient awe. *Brosnað enta geweorc.*

5

During a war that would become a footnote to later wars, a Russian army seized the city of Edirne. The retreating Ottomans set fire to their stores of ammunition, which they had kept in the warehouses of the old imperial palace. The palace exploded for three days. Four hundred years earlier, the vast complex had been squarely at the center of things, a capital of sorts, but then Istanbul became Istanbul and Edirne fell in prestige. Perhaps feeling neglected, it decided to put on a show. BOOM went the roofs of the eighteen baths. BOOM went the kitchens, fire flailing through their chimneys. BOOM water towers crashed down on the gates. BOOM latticed balconies crumbled into courtyards. BOOM fish leapt from ornamental pools, blinking. BOOM flames ate up silk carpets and sacks of grain. BOOM the half-walls and spy holes and velvet corridors that once saw viziers ghosting and princes tussling and sultans seething now heaved in ash up to the sky.

Other parts of Edirne, where people still lived, were also destroyed in the Russian siege. In the chaotic aftermath of the city's conquest, people came to the ruined palace to scavenge materials for their own homes, grateful for a higher quality of rubble. The sultans bring war upon our heads, at least they can patch up our walls. When the Ottomans retook Edirne some time later, little remained of the old palace, only a handful of denuded buildings and one solitary bath.

A court official was horrified by the pillage. It's one thing for boorish foreigners to stomp all over our monuments, quite another for our subjects to do the same. He took it upon himself to search for traces of the palace in the homes of Edirne's people. It was unlikely they would willfully return the palatial bits, and in any case, he resolved not to make any strong demands. Instead, the official made a catalogue of his discoveries, a list to remember the grandeur.

In the home of a saddler, filled with the leather breath of the man's work, the official saw pearl-dappled slabs of marble glowing by the stove. In the home of a scrivener, turtles from the sultan's gardens roamed across the floor with candles strapped to their shells. In the bakeries, the assistants fanned bread fresh from the ovens with peacock feathers. The official poked about churches and the few places of the Jewish quarter, but the people ate their porridge and asked for the news as if theirs was an unchanged world out of time. In the camp of Gypsies on the city's outskirts, they whispered children to sleep using pictures from ancient illuminated manuscripts to tell Gypsy stories. In an apothecary, a water pipe gurgled through ivory mouths shaped like Chinese dragons. In the marketplaces, traders exchanged coins that had not been used in centuries. The operators of Edirne's telegraph post sat on cushions worthy of queens. In every house high and low, the official's feet passed silently over the blue rumor of tile.

A sentry at the main city gate took the official by the hand to his guard post. It seemed like an impossible structure, assembled from fragments of the palace. The ribbed, conical plume of a kitchen chimney sat at its top. Inside, the official could make out the corners of fountains, the grooves of hydraulic channels, gossamer stone screens, the buffed marble of a sultan's grand dais. The sentry knocked against walls of tiled flowers. You see, he said, it was built to last.

6

Afanasii Nikitin, a Russian merchant, didn't particularly like India. He arrived in Gujarat in 1471 with a stallion (to trade), a journal (to record), anxious Christian beliefs (to fret about in solitude), and his penis. He struggled to acquire goods of interest to Russians, likely because he had little to offer in return (Russians had yet to invent the MiG). People stared at him on the streets and were amused by his skin color. He thought Indians were black and shameless, a prescient insight then, since so many Indians now deride their own countrymen as black and shameless.

In the account he left us he chooses to spend an inordinate amount of time describing the cheapness of Indian women. You can have them for two coppers, he says, but if you really like them and want to throw your money to the wind, give them five. That was the generous extent of his wanderlust. Afanasii reports hearsay that in China, the women pay to sleep with white foreigners in the hope that they will give birth to white children. He sketches the outline of the Indian Ocean from Cambay to Cathay, defining each point by the value of its tradable commodities and the ease of sex—a perfectly male mercantilism.

Over the course of his narrative, one gets the sense that Afanasii might have converted to Islam. Certain holy invocations and sayings seem translated directly from Persian or Arabic into

Russian. He asks for forgiveness for taking an Arabic name. That is the fault of travel, he says, it upsets your moral foundations. He consoles himself in his constant belief in one god. When he accompanies a sultan in his attack on a Hindu kingdom, Afanasii relishes giving accounts of men killed, elephants stampeded, horses toppled, towns sacked, temples destroyed.

Nowhere in his diary is there any suggestion that he missed being home.

A stallion's letter to Afanasii Nikitin

For me, you were given some sum. Not once did you stroke my mane, even though you liked admiring me from behind and feeling my muscular haunches. I know. My eyes are on the sides of my head, you see. I have a better sense of before and after than you do. Before me, there was only a man and his horse. After me will come textiles, coins, pepper, more coins, gems, slaves, more pepper, and even more coins; you will do well in Hormuz and Ethiopia, be penniless by the time you get to Trebizond, shiver in Crimea. As you die of pneumonia on your way home to Tver, remember that at the beginning we were lonely together. You tried to ride me once, but fell off.

An Indian prostitute's letter to Afanasii Nikitin

Holding your bald and beaded head in my hands, I feel the texture of a boiled potato, the skin crinkling, soft yellow flesh lifting to steam. But potatoes have not yet arrived in my country from the new world, so let me say this instead: You are a yam, and I will eat you if I must.

7

When Odysseus returns to his own land, he carries the bloody world of the *Iliad* to Ithaca. He slaughters the suitors and lynches their chambermaid collaborators ("for a little while they twitched their feet," the poet tells us, "but that did not last long"), and then, after one further skirmish, is restored to wife and throne. After so long on alien seas, he has finally come home.

But the real ending of his tale is left to the imagination. Many chapters previously, the prophet Teiresias tells Odysseus that once home, he must carry an oar deep into the hinterland until he reaches a place where the people have not heard of the sea. At that point, he should plant the oar in the ground and offer a big, meaty sacrifice to Poseidon, thereby making a final peace with the prickly deity who tossed him around the Mediterranean.

The Homeric poet does not describe this last voyage, but grants us the leisure of its imagining. Eventually, after some time at home Odysseus misses his former solitude. He doesn't explain to Penelope why he must leave—the two find talking to each other difficult—only that a prophecy needs fulfilling. She makes no protest, and wraps a bundle for him. In the morning, he sets off down Ithaca's dust paths, oar over his shoulder, a few dogs at his heels. The dogs stay with him, panting alongside through sheepfolds and meadows, until they come to the normal limit of their master's rambling. He crosses over a stream, or into a pass that slopes toward the uplands, or through some other crease in the countryside understandable to the hounds as a border. Nuzzling his knees, they look up at Odysseus. Go home, he says, and strides on. Whimpering, the dogs drop away.

A few days into his walking, he begins to question the people he meets. What am I carrying? They think this leathered man has lost his mind. He must be a drifter addled by the sun. It's an oar, they say with concern, why on earth are you walking around with an oar? Which way is the sea? Odysseus asks. They point and watch Odysseus turn in the opposite direction and walk on.

How can it be that there are people who don't know about the sea? he thinks as his sandals fray and his face bristles anew. Everybody knows the sea and its gods and spirits, just as they know the land, revere Demeter with her holy pigs and snakes. Duality exists in all things, there is no earth without sea, no sea without earth. This is an impossible quest, he thinks, Poseidon is toying with me again.

The oar begins to feel like an anchor. To distract himself from its weight, he makes his shoulder a groove and waves the oar behind him, as if he was rowing himself onward. Travelers on the narrowing trails ask him if he is looking for the coast. He shakes his head. The deeper he journeys beyond the regular swellings of villages and towns, the easier it becomes to lose the path. Just like the sea, it is possible for the land to bear no trace of the passage of people. Odysseus is comforted one night when he sees a campfire across an empty Thracian valley, fragile as the lantern hanging from a distant ship. He lays the oar down and lets the earth move in waves beneath his back till he falls asleep.

When wolves come for him one dusk, he uses the oar to brush them aside. He scuttles bandits, too, swinging the oar at their necks, jabbing the blade into their ribs. The oar is the symbol of the sea; it marks Odysseus as the emissary of Poseidon.

And yet it is made from the strongest wood, solid enough to crack the heads of any pirates.

His sandals fray beyond repair. He walks on, barefoot. The answers to his questions grow more tenuous and vague, as if they do not describe an object, but rather the idea of an object. Odysseus feels hopeful. Meeting a traveler or coming into a scraggly farmstead, he has to scour all the vocabulary of his roaming, all the memories of strangers and foreign slaves to ask simply, What is this? After some confusion, his interlocutors explain that it is an oar, a paddle, an instrument of water. They mime the gliding shape of a trireme, the breathing of sails.

Deflated, Odysseus carries on. At night, he feels the sudden urge to break the oar and burn it. He picks it up and raises it over his knee. Its shaft is smoothed and worn from his long touch, its butt rounded to a soft bump. His sweat polishes the wood. The skin of his fingers feels like bark. He cannot destroy such an intimate thing. He sleeps that night with his arms around the oar, his cheek pressed against the blade.

A few days later, Odysseus arrives at a grass plain that stretches far to the horizon, interrupted only by an archipelago of mountains. At an oasis way station, he asks the travelers and merchants about the oar. They speak no common tongue so the people take the oar off his shoulder to show Odysseus how it is used. This is a winnowing shovel, one woman explains through her motions. She carries the oar to a pile of grain, which she lifts into the breeze. You use it to separate the grain from the chaff, and even better, to cleanse the grain of weevils. Odysseus smiles as the air fills with wheat dust. No, no, the baker interrupts, give it to me, I'll show you. He takes the oar to his ovens and slides it under a pillow of flatbread. With a turn of his wrists and a swivel of his torso, he plops the steaming bread in front of Odysseus. The baker ends his performance by brandishing the oar like a spear and stamping his feet. Between mouthfuls of delicious bread, Odysseus cannot stop laughing.

In exchange for a few bronze clasps of jewelry, the hero acquires a ram (Teiresias told him to sacrifice a ram, a bull, and a wild boar to Poseidon, but Odysseus decides that the ram will just have to do). He goes into the steppe at night dragging the ram behind him. Under the bright constellations, he plants the oar in the ground. He closes his eyes to offer a prayer to the sea god. For a moment, the wind over the grass sounds like the wind over the sea, the way he has heard it and forgotten it and heard it again, skimming foam from the caps, chasing shadows on the water, cooling his blistered cheeks. The ram looks at the oar with ugly suspicion and bleats. Off to Poseidon with you, Odysseus says. He slits the animal's throat. The bowl Penelope packed for him is so small that it overflows almost immediately with the creature's blood. A red pool forms at the base of the oar. Odysseus completes his prayers and the necessary carving, and then lies down. He wills himself to dream of his wandering years, of the pleasures and miseries of the mariner: Calypso's legs, the roaring whirlpools, the blood sunsets over orange waters, and then that eternal terror, when sails tear, oars snap, hulls shiver, when the great beamed mast topples over the deck and sailors shed the membrane that keeps them from the hateful sea.

When he wakes, there is the taste of salt on his lips. It is strange to walk without the oar over his shoulder. He makes his way to the oasis, which is not in the direction he remembered it to be. I've grown even older, he thinks. The mountains, too, seem to have drifted off their moorings. I thought those were to the north, not the south. At the oasis, he asks the people there if they could remind him which direction he came from. They shrug. When the grass ends, they explain, there is only forest all around. Odysseus grows frantic. Which way is the sea? he mimes with every possible contortion of his body. They do not understand. He speaks, using all the words he can think of that mean sea in each language that has passed through his head. One of the words reaches shore. Sea, a man says, sea! Yes, sea, Odysseus grasps his hand, which way is the sea? The man smiles. He gestures at the infinite steppe. Sea.

8

In the upper reaches of a medieval European map—one of those beautiful Italian planispheres drawn from Arab traditions of cosmography, with the south at the top and north at the bottom—bobs an enormous Indian caravel. You could miss the detail and think it is only another European ship, another plucky foot soldier in the white man's conquest of the sea. The inscription tells another story. The ship is an "Indian junk," built with four masts, housing sixty cabins' worth of merchants. Though large, it was so ingeniously designed that it needed only one tiller. Its navigators didn't require compasses because they had in their ranks a full-time astrologer, who would steady himself on the deck with his astrolabe and shout out directions from the stars.

This Indian vessel in 1420 sailed to the southern tip of Africa, called Diab by the monkish cartographer. From there, the ship journeyed two thousand miles west. Finding only water and wind—not even ice or penguins or the dribbled little islands of the South Atlantic—the Indians decided to turn back. The astrologer had lost his bearings. In this way, Indians missed the best chance they had to discover Indians.

9

The earliest documents we have in the now-extinct Sogdian language come from a bundle of undelivered letters. Archaeologists in the 1970s found this ancient mailbag in the ruins of a watchtower in western China. Nearly two thousand years ago, the tower was besieged and burnt to the ground. The letters survived, preserved for centuries in the dry desert.

Of the poor postman, we know nothing. Presumably, he went up in flames along with the tower. Or he never made it to the tower, was stripped of his mailbag and gutted by the Chinese border garrison. Or he was swept up in the attack on the tower and died on its ramparts. All sorts of sad fates could have engulfed him. Letterless nomads had sacked the capital and destroyed many cities. Rebellions rippled through the teetering empire. The postman was carrying missives out from a devastated land.

Like so many of the liminal peoples of the world, the Sogdians were traders. They settled across the expanse of the silk route in communities tethered to their homeland in Central Asia, the twin cities of Samarkand and Bukhara. Caught up in the frenzy in China, they wrote home.

Here, a merchant's representative reports to headquarters of the unfolding debacle. Here, a trader, who does not expect to return home, asks that the interest accumulated in one of his deposits be allotted to a certain orphan in Samarkand.

Here, a woman complains bitterly to her husband that she and her daughter have not heard from him in ages. To pay his debts, she says, they have been forced to work as servants in a Chinese household. She begins the letter in the conventional way: *To my noble lord husband, blessing and homage on bended knee, as is offered to the gods.* She ends in unflinching rebuke: *I would rather be a pig's or a dog's wife than yours!*

Here, the same woman writes to her mother. No one will allow her daughter and her to leave, she says, no one will guarantee their passage out of China. She has only one source of comfort and hope: a charitable priest recently offered her a camel.

Here, a trader informs the chief merchant that a colleague sent into the Chinese interior eight years ago has not been heard from for three.

A year must have been shorter then than it is now. The greater the speed of our news, the slower the speed of our time. Like ours, the Sogdian calendar was three hundred and sixty-five days long. Like us, they kept four seasons. In the last month of winter, they spent a day tearing at their faces in mourning for the dead. On certain days in spring, thieves and crooks were allowed to bring counterfeit goods to the market and sell them in the open air. The Sogdians counted their years in the reigns of kings, which means they never had to count for very long.

And yet no stretch of time feels as long as the wait for a message. If they were not killed, or further displaced and dispossessed, these letter writers would have watched the arrival of every rider with expectation. They would wonder why no response ever came. They might pray. In lantern-lit nights, they wrote more hopeful letters. Somebody took those away, dropping them into the world in the scuffing of boots, the sound of hooves, the slow shrinking of a caravan from lumps to nothing. If anybody could hear the absolute silence of the desert, it was the letter writers.

10

Siberia is so big there are still rivers without names. A family raced out of time into the hugeness of the taiga. They dug out a home in the wooded hills, hundreds of kilometers away from the nearest human beings. Over the years, the things they brought with them from the modern world—a kettle, a pot, salt—all melted away. They read the Bible by firelight. In seasons of plenty, they ate potato patties. In famine, they ate bark and leaves. When they were bored, they assembled in the dark cabin and revealed to each other the splendor of their dreams.

After his wife died of starvation, the old father took to watching the night sky. He noticed with surprise the growing number of stars fleeing across the blue. These were satellites.

Soviet geologists discovered the family in 1978. They watched from a distance and then left gifts on the threshold. Little by little, they established ties with the family. Soon, the father and his children began to troop down to the geologists' camp. One son was absorbed by the wonders of the sawmill, its perfect planes of wood. The rest of them watched TV. The father looked at the images through his fingers, whispering all the time, This is forbidden, this is forbidden, this is forbidden. His children would watch for a while and then run around the corner to pray for forgiveness. Then they watched some more.

Within three years, almost all of the family were dead, killed by the hardship of their remote lives now that they had come into an understanding of their remoteness. The father and lone surviving daughter lived together for a while. When he died, she buried him with the help of the geologists.

Her story ends predictably, not in narrative but in image. The geologists last saw her standing "like a statue" in her forest, willing them to leave her alone. Go on, go on, she said with movements of her stony chin.

Let's not leave her there, memorialized in the stoic expression of her strange life. Let's say this instead. On her own, she built a coracle out of reeds and branches. She filled it with her family's things, the things they kept, the things they made. With her hands and legs she rowed down the nameless tributary that she had drunk from her whole life, south into Mongolia. There, she cleared a small patch of forest and made her little home. In her last summers, she came down into the high pastures and befriended the herders. They let her help mind the children. She told the Mongolian kids her dreams, and they, in their own way, told her theirs.

CULTURAL PROPERTY

It was forged heavy in ornament, light in bite. Perhaps the blacksmith—dark with sorrow for the loss of his lord—mocked up a quick one to join the thane's passage to the next world. Centuries under the earth made the sword vegetal, the shaft mushroomed with warp, the pommel barnacled beyond rust. Perhaps it had a name: Shadow-sting, Iron-strong, Doom's Face, Edge of the World. Or perhaps it was nameless, just another sword in a time of swords, when men slopped drunk between the boards and the winter drafts tugged at the ankles of the slaves.

I kneel over my discovery. I am by myself but for a few colleagues roaming the edges of the site, taking the day's last measurements, packing up their things. Tracy yells that the bus is leaving. I've chosen to walk back every day of this dig, so she allows me my crouched silence. I listen to her crunch over the lip of the excavation, to the hydraulic embrace of the shuttle. It rumbles away with its cargo of professionals and students. A seagull nuzzles the sand in front of me, searching for crabs. I give it a conspiratorial nod.

Between the fenced site and our shorefront hotel lies over a mile of forlorn beach, spat at by the glacial disdain of the North Sea. I climb down to the sand and pull out my mobile phone. Yarmouth Harbour's cranes cobweb the horizon. Wind turbines hover over the surf. I ring a number. A voice answers, Where? I explain where. Good, stay there. I hang up. A tanker shrinks into the distance along the old sea road to Rotterdam. So many people have been here before me, teeth chattering, in centuries of damp woolen cloaks and rough-cobbled boots, looking across the water with dread and longing.

The sun sinks behind me and I watch my shadow reach toward the sea and disappear. With the toe of my shoe, I trace my name in the sand in every script I know, three dots over the *sheen* in Persian, a *C* for the *K* in Old English, the emphatic Hindi bridge over the top, before wiping them clear and starting again. I am nervous. Soon, dark vans will pull up to the excavation site. The security guard won't have time to react. When offered so unimaginable a bribe, he'll throw up his hands in happy surrender. Do as you please, sirs, and Yes, I've angled the cameras in other directions, and Don't worry, I'll record over the tapes to be certain, and Would you like a cup of tea? The men will be too professional for tea. Within minutes, they'll have the sword and any other objects in its vicinity treated and contained, ready for transoceanic travel. I will get a handshake and a phone call to confirm the delivery. Someone will give me an envelope of cash that I will neither deposit nor spend. I don't do this for the money.

Exile should be kind to the sword, even though it will settle in a country dangerously humid for Anglo-Saxon iron. It will live in a humming climate-controlled case, organized into some meaningful narrative: "Warfare in European Late Antiquity," "Beowulf and His Age," or a hopeful crowd-pleaser, "Primitive Britain." In any case, visitors will probably not notice the curators' scheme, the careful framing of the sword within its social and temporal milieu, its echoes on tapestries or in priestly illuminations. No one really *sees* anything in museums. They'll come from Chandigarh and Bhopal, Mysore and Mathura, Coimbatore and Siliguri, snapping pictures on their phones, loudly texting, trailing the debris of their nagging conversations (Idiot child, why did we bring you here if you don't look, look, look at this thing?) and *channa chur* (try as they might, the guards can do nothing to control snacking; Indian museumgoers are the deftest smugglers). They will look at the sword and say, Oh, wouldn't that be a terrible way to go, or, It's not fair to judge, but don't you think our swords are more elegant? or, It really makes you think how bleak England was, or, It really makes you think how bleak the world is. If they read the caption (they won't), they will learn that the item was excavated for and is the exclusive property of the Nalanda Museum of Art and Global Culture, Patna. All the bleakness is ours.

My task is simple enough. I just have to wait, ensure a safe and smooth transaction, keep the security guard happy in coming weeks, and carry on digging as if nothing ever happened. The sea sludges against the rusting shore. I imagine my colleagues eating cheese toast in the hotel's lounge and watching *Question Time* with David Dimbleby, "this week from Basingstoke." Life can be comfortable amid the ruins.

A shape approaches along the beach. I thrust my hands into my pockets, sink my neck into my collar, and contemplate the water. As it draws near, I yawn. Nothing to see here, just an Indian archaeologist communing with Poseidon, move along. The footsteps slow and scuff to a halt. I turn. Thought I would find you here, Tracy says.

It's mesmerizing.

And stupidly cold. She pulls a hip flask from her jacket. The whiskey scrapes the back of my head. Mind if I sit? she asks, crossing her legs on the sand.

I look at her through my teeth.

You may as well make yourself comfortable. She smooths the sand beside her. I sit. She looms next to me in the dark, an immovable block of stone.

The clouds shift, and a sliver of the moon slips through the gray bank. Tracy glows. You know, the rest of them find you very endearing. Such a romantic, all this lingering and willful solitude. She lifts one knee and twists closer. They don't know that you're actually such an inexplicable grouch. She kisses me and rakes my teeth with her malty tongue.

Do they know you've come out here? Do they know about us?

About us? What about us? No, she says. Maybe Tim. And Liz, too—she's giving me the evil eye. I reckon she fancies you. A fine eyebrow arches at me. What would it matter if they all did know?

It's deeply unprofessional.

Don't be ridiculous.

It is. It is. Who would ever send a couple on a dig? Who would trust them with funds or take their receipts?

Couples work together all the time.

Incorrect.

Are you calling us a couple?

I grunt, a bit lost.

Don't get ahead of yourself, she says, you're going to have to put in more time before you use words like that.

We kiss again and within me deep down, beneath many strata of cultivation, I begin to feel the rumblings of an ancient fear.

Listen, I say, this is silly. Meet me at the hotel. In the warmth. Under the covers.

With a mug of hot chocolate? I quite like it out here with you.

I'll meet you there in a bit. I promise. I just need some privacy to make a few phone calls.

To who?

I want to talk to my mother.

Your mother? It must be two in the morning in India.

She's traveling, giving lectures in the States.

Okay, that's fine. Tracy makes no move to go.

Well?

I'll just sit here, I'm not going to eavesdrop. You can walk away from me if you wish. But don't go too far. I like looking at you.

Tracy.

What, it's not like you're trying to take a piss. I won't hear a word. Go on.

I take a swig of whiskey and rise into the wind. Once I feel a safe distance away, I redial my last call. There's a problem, I say. It's too late, the voice replies, they're almost there. Make the problem go away. The line cuts out, but I keep the phone held to my face. I look at Tracy, a green and black bundle on the ashen sand. She waves. The first time we kissed we were in Scotland in the dregs of the summer, bumping out of a pub into the greasy glare of a chip shop, then to the back of a miraculous taxi. She didn't mind my love of the drunken procession, my childish habits, if anything she seemed to find them endearing. I was flattered, and surprised. She had spent the evening needling me, first about my overpronunciation, then the schoolboy side-parting of my haircut, and finally my vocation. You don't regret the strange life you've chosen, clawing at these marshes with us? Maybe I should have been born in India, and you here. I told her I'd come to Britain so many years ago for the incomparable weather and food, of course—and for the women. She smiled.

Some of us are glad for your poor taste. In the taxi, she traced the calluses on my palms as I devoured her neck. She spooned around me in the morning and whispered into my hair. Well, now you should have one less thing to regret.

I call the number again. Listen, you have to call it off, I say, this is an intractable problem, a problem with no solution, a problem your people won't be able to bribe away. Who is it? the voice asks. A colleague. Can he be persuaded of the virtues of the project? No, definitely no, she wouldn't understand. You have ten minutes . . . persuade him, or make him go away.

I return to Tracy. She has kicked off her boots and is crinkling her toes. I need you to go back to the hotel. I require time to myself, I say.

What's wrong? You've been alone long enough. Her arm is around my waist, holding me with a strange strength.

If you asked this of me, I'd oblige you.

I wouldn't ask this of you. I wouldn't avoid you. I wouldn't look at you with such guilty eyes each morning. She puts both her arms around me. I want you to relax. You can talk to me. And Christ, if you can't talk to me, just shut up and be with me.

I don't expect you to understand, Tracy, but I need some space. Please just leave me be. I'll come to you later.

She releases me. You're intolerable. Go.

I'm sorry.

Go to the hotel. I'd like to be pouty and moody and sit in the mizzle and think sad thoughts. Go have space in your hotel room. Scratch your balls and watch *EastEnders* and wait for me to knock on your door tonight. Or not knock. She leans back on her elbows, hair lashing from her hood, lips set in a granite challenge. Her eyes look away from me to the big dark of the sea.

Can I explain it to her? Maybe. I'll say, It's not theft, I found the sword, or, Perhaps it's rightfully the property of the University of East Anglia, but what good will it do there, unknown in a basement? or, Why can't we own fragments of your past, since you've taken so much of ours? She'll call it petty revenge, and there is nothing so outmoded as revenge. It's an argument, I'll say, it's an argument about how to be global. We want our own universal museums. She'll shake her head: I had no idea you were such a nationalist. I'm not a nationalist, I'm just Indian. Fine, she'll say, but why steal? Why not arrange loans? It's not enough, we want to own it just as you own ours. Fine, she'll say, but then why don't you buy? You can legally buy artifacts for your whatever museum. At what extortionate price? And who would even sell? Nobody feels more entitled to their own history than the English. I'll lift my chin. Can you imagine what would happen if we shipped the Sutton Hoo Helmet or the Staffordshire Hoard to India? There would be riots. National Trust volunteers clad in cardigans, armed with pitchforks. Maybe she would smile at that. I hope she would smile.

No, she wouldn't accept it. She would reject this conviction in objects, the worship of the unknowable past. After all, we have seen what lies beneath. For months together we have squelched in bogs up and down the country, hunched over in the rain, searching for the bones of the dead. When found, they emerge from small graves, brittle and coated with peat, more frightened than frightening. Often, the skeletal bits are joined by other things: shards of pottery, animal ashes, warped blades. Historians and geneticists take these pieces and build a shadowy world of mead halls and longships, a Dark Age of piety and blood that seems all the more surreal to her when faced with our daily universe of mud. She is alarmed by the speed with which one theory replaces another. She finds no solace in the indifference of bone, in the permanence of remains. She thinks the cliché that "nothing lasts forever" is false. Lots of things last forever, if only as reminders of their nothingness. But they aren't nothing, I told her once. Yeah, she said, then let me know when they're something.

She looks at me now with the patient gaze I know so well, that even, unruffled way she examines our finds. I want to hold her. She thinks her diligence can unveil my secrets, too.

I'm meeting someone, I say.

Who? Who are you meeting?

Someone else.

She looks away and with one finger searches in the sand. You weren't talking to your mother, she says.

I wasn't.

Who is she? Who? She endures my silence and gets to her feet. Were you going to tell me?

I didn't know there was anything to be said. My fingers move behind her ear through her hair to the point where jaw meets neck. She holds my wrist for an instant and then throws it away. She stomps off toward the hotel in her socks. I gather up her boots. When I look up, she has paused in the distance. I think she is looking back at me, huddled, clutching her shoes. The stray beam of a car wheels over us. For an instant, it seems that she is growing larger, that she returns to me, limned and stretched with light. But in the sudden rush of darkness that follows, I know she is gone.

I think of the original owner of the sword, the dead thane yet to be uncovered, slumbering somewhere else in the site, his skull peppered with rings that had held the braids of his hair, teeth sticking like chips of wood from the jaw, the torques circling loose and empty on the skeleton's arms. There would be other objects besides. The tattered bridle of a favorite horse. The rusted clasps of drinking and hunting horns. The bones of others: a wife from Frisia, a consort from Birka, a slave from Cymru, the strangled privilege of other times and other places. All these things were once his and his alone, without question or remorse.

Moments later, I hear tires crunching on gravel. My phone rings. I wait a few beats and then answer.

THE PHALANX

WESTERN ANATOLIA, 190 B.C.

Seen from afar, the collision of brigades of spearmen looks almost gentle. The lines don't rush into one another, but slow as they near, straightening. Losing shape means death in the clash of phalanxes. When the sides are just a few spear lengths apart, there is a pause, a collective breath, before the impact of shafts and shields. A general watching from above or from the side may know intimately what goes on in the fray, all the shoving and thrusting, but he cannot see it. At that distance, the violence of a phalanx is invisible. Its front ranks lock in place and begin to nudge the enemy. The men behind bob on their heels, unsure when they'll have some killing to do. The largest phalanxes run fifty deep. The men at the very back plant their spears in the ground and strain over the shoulders of their comrades to see a battle happening far away.

A red-bearded soldier turns to his neighbor, a clean-shaven man with a delicate mole on his upper lip. What do you reckon? he says.

The usual, the other replies, ten minutes, fifteen tops. The two men stand lightly, with their knees bent, ready to push forward or step back as required. Hundreds of helmets crowd between them and the front, where men press against each other and squelch in the blood. The key to winning is making a breach in the enemy line. Once that happens, the enemy's resolve crumbles and the tight ranks of spearmen unspool, scattering soldiers from the battlefield.

I don't think it will be easy, the red-beard says, look, back in the distance, they've brought their own elephants.

Our elephants are much bigger, the man with the mole says, and more aggressive.

Are they?

Yes, I'm told North African elephants don't have the same warlike spirit . . . apparently the climate makes them lazy.

Still, it's an awful lot of elephants.

If you must worry, you should worry about their skirmishers.

Why, are we being fired on?

I'm not sure, but it's only a matter of time before they try to spook us with javelins.

What about from our side, the red-beard wonders, where are our skirmishers?

The Elymaean bowmen or the Cyrtian slingers?

Actually, I was thinking of the Mysian archers.

Somewhere on the right flank.

Those Mysians keep dancing boys in their camp.

When did you go?

I didn't, but I heard from somebody else . . . He was passing by at night and he heard the sound of pipes and tamburs, and he saw these soft-limbed boys prancing around the fires.

The further west you go, the man with the mole says, the stranger people get . . . We were all better off staying put in Syria.

A horn blares along the enemy line. A burst of the enemy's battle chant reaches them before vanishing, like the finger of a wave. Somewhere to their left, the tail leader shouts at his men, urging them to sing a reply. Alalalalalai, the men cry, alalalalalai . . . we commend ourselves to the god of war.

They're putting up a fight, the man with the mole says.

I told you, I told you they meant business.

We've barely moved forward at all.

You're taller than me, what's happening on the flanks?

Climb on my shoulders and have a look.

Don't joke, the red-beard says, and kicks his neighbor.

It's all dust, my friend, all dust . . . I can barely see the end of our brigade . . . Oh, there to the right, if you must know, we're guarded by three turreted war elephants.

I heard the king is leading the horse cavalry today.

He's always "leading" the cavalry.

It's a fine sight, isn't it, when he rides out in the lionskin of his ancestors and barrels through the lines.

Half the time, he's chasing down irregulars, leaving the real fighting to us.

What I wouldn't give to be in the cavalry and not this damn phalanx.

You'll never be rich enough to serve in the cavalry.

I can steal what I need, the red-beard insists, all of it, armor, lance, horse, even the money for a squire.

Then what's the problem?

You know what it is.

Hah . . . oh yes, you can't ride.

No, I just don't do horses.

Ride a donkey then.

Every time I get on the animal, the thing knows I'm unworthy of it . . . it always chucks me off.

The first javelins and arrows race out of the dust and thud around them. The men in the back rows lean their long spears forward, making a thicket over the men further front. They feel the percussion of missiles knocking against this latticed roof, the bolts splintering, dropping timidly on helms and cuirasses.

Inevitably, some arrows fly through and hit home. The men shift in their rows and adjust to fill the opened spaces.

I'm telling you, the man with the mole says, we should pull back to the Taurus.

If the king's armies don't take this land, then Rome will have it.

Well, then let Rome have it . . . we have enough provinces to take care of.

I didn't think you were so naïve . . . this land will be a buffer for the king's core provinces.

We should just build a wall.

A wall?

Yes, to keep out the Romans and all these western tribes and warlords.

That doesn't strike me as very practical.

You know the story about the king's great forebear Alexander, how he built a wall to fence off the barbarians and demons at the edge of the world.

Well, that was then, this is now.

Right, and now we run the risk of dying here because the blessed king thinks he's a Persian emperor.

Shut up and push. Alalalalalai! Alalalalalai!

The men hitch the shields to their shoulders and press whoever is in front of them. The phalanx compresses into its densest form, a rectangle of packed flesh and metal. Over a thousand spearmen bear down on the enemy brigade. It steps backward slowly, absorbing the pressure. Somewhere in the dust ahead there are men stepping over bodies, stabbing under and over shields, their grunting faces kept from the grunting faces of their foes by the enamel of two bronze plates.

The front rank is where ambitious warriors aspire to be, the only place where others will notice their merit and remember their actions. Those men spit and shove and gasp for air, pinned by the forces of two irreconcilable directions. The youngest soldiers stand just behind the front rows, gulping hard, their knuckles pale. Veterans of varying degrees of worth form the rear. Their main role is to make sure the youngsters in the middle don't flee. They also set the rhythm of the pushing, that great occupation of the phalanx. Only if all the men push together will their straining be of use.

The forward momentum slows and then stops. They're not breaking, the red-beard says. The youths in the middle crane their necks back and yell, Stop it, stop pushing so hard, you're crushing us . . . Can't you see it's not working? The phalanx loosens and resumes the work of prying for gaps in the enemy line.

You would think a brigade so deep wouldn't have this kind of trouble, the man with the mole says.

These Romans must be good at pushing back, the red-beard says, strong fellows.

I suppose.

I heard from somebody that in their victories, the Romans are often outnumbered . . . they know how to win against the odds.

That's what everybody says, it's rarely true.

Isn't that what the Romans did to the king last year?

Rumors and legends . . . bards always say X stood bravely against Y, outnumbered five to one, and X still came out the victor.

Maybe that's just the mark of good tactics, or maybe some peoples are in fact stronger than others.

Nonsense, it's guff, bunkum . . . you know how war works, the winning side is the one that has more people pushing.

The red-beard splits in a smile. So you're predicting a glorious day for us, he says. One day, you'll go back home and you'll tell your kids, "I was there, at Mağnisa."

Oh shut up.

"I was there at the back of the phalanx with all the old scoundrels and we pushed, oh how we pushed, until somewhere ahead of us, the flower of Rome wilted and the legionaries ran away."

You know I don't have kids.

Well, your wife might at this point.

Very funny.

And you'll tell your wife's kids, "That was a rare day, a fine day, the day Antiochus, King of the East, stopped the tyrannical advance of Rome."

Yes, yes, well the irony is that if we somehow come out on the winning side today, you will go home and actually talk to your brats just like that.

It's true, I might . . . don't blame me for having some esprit de corps.

The man with a mole turns to his red-bearded neighbor. In the dust and swelter of the phalanx, it can be difficult to hold the gaze of a person even so near. Their helmets hang low over the brow, shading the eyes. How come you've never told me their names?

Whose?

Your children's.

They are young, still too young to have their names spoken with any confidence.

Is that the custom where you're from?

The red-beard shakes his head. It is just my custom.

At what point then would you feel ready to talk about them?

Children should talk about the deeds of their fathers . . . fathers should not talk about their children.

The tail leader begins to sing a war hymn. All the soldiers of the rear join in and the chant floods forward, where it crashes into the din of the front line. Up there, the occasional would-be hero jumps over the shields and tries to disrupt the enemy line. He ends up stabbed and beaten into the trough of gore separating the two armies.

Poor fools, the man with a mole says, we outgrew that kind of bravery years ago . . . courage is probably the most overrated virtue.

Well, it takes courage to be where we are.

I don't know . . . we probably won't have to thrust a spear in anger today.

Still, we're here, on the battlefield, where anything can happen, our lives at the mercy of the fates.

The ancients had it right . . . Gilgamesh and Humbaba, Rustam and Sohrab, Hector and Achilles . . . the ancients made war the arena of heroes . . . it was about the glory of the leaders, who wanted the war in the first place, who had everything to gain and everything to lose . . . a battle was decided by that individual contest; it wasn't about the multitude, mobilizing the peasants, emptying the towns, flinging us poor sods at each other, a people against another people.

I thought there were thousands of men fighting at Troy.

If our leaders were truly great men, it would just be the king and the Roman general, in single combat, and they'd leave the rest of us out of it.

You're acting as if you have no stake in the fight.

Exactly, I have none.

But that's not true at all, you have as much interest as I do in the spoils of war.

Hah, the "spoils of war."

Think about all the bracelets and earrings you can bring back to your wife . . . maybe you can even find her a slave or two.

She has enough baubles.

After so long away from her, you'd probably do well to give her some more.

Why do you always bring up my wife?

Because it's funny that somebody as restless as you is married.

Well, what do you expect . . . we're all married until we aren't.

A wind gusts through. For a moment, the roiling dust clears. The battle spreads out before them in wavering lines, bristling hedgerows of spearmen, archers shooting, slingers pelting volley after volley, elephants stomping, messengers galloping behind with news from the far wings of the melee. And yet even in the midst of this frenzy, there are so many men fidgeting in their spots, doing nothing at all. The wind relents and the dust closes on the phalanx, hiding the rest of the field.

You know, Socrates served in a phalanx.

Who?

The philosopher, lived in the west ages ago . . . even you've heard of him.

A philosopher in the phalanx, why not . . . we have musicians, tinkers, weavers, masons, sheep traders, poets . . . may as well chuck a philosopher in there, too.

Socrates compared his commitment to philosophy, that search for truth, to the commitment men have to each other in the phalanx, the perseverance and resolve, fight till the end, all that.

The guy didn't die fighting, right?

No, he drank poison.

Well, then he couldn't have been all that committed, could he . . . he knew as much as us that when the line breaks, you turn and run and run and run.

Do you remember that time, the man with a mole asks, in the eastern campaign when we were green, when the line broke and we fled?

Of course, like an idiot you threw away your shield.

I know, for shame . . . you saved my honor then, whatever it's worth.

I had to run back and get it for you . . . can you imagine me now, with this belly and these angry knees, trying to carry both our shields as we're being chased down by a pack of Indians?

Was it Indians?

Was it not?

That far in the east, who knows.

Anyway, there you were, a twig of a man . . . I'll never forget how fast you ran.

Cowardice is a part of life, you can't be brave if you've never known fear.

You just said you don't believe in bravery.

No, I said bravery is overrated . . . and for that matter, cowardice is underrated.

Spoken like a true warrior.

Better alive as a coward than dead as a hero . . . you know who said that?

Who?

Achilles to Odysseus in Hades.

Okay, I can't read but I do listen, and that's not what he actually said.

Then do tell, oh bard, what did Achilles actually say?

Better to be a peasant in the world above than a king in the world below.

Oh right, maybe he did say that.

See, it changes the meaning completely . . . would you rather be a peasant in this life than a king in Hades?

Of course not, I wake up every morning to say thanks that my mornings aren't the mornings of a peasant.

Exactly . . . like so many princelings, Achilles had absolutely no idea what he was talking about.

Drums sound in the distance, horns blare. The ranks of the phalanx tighten. The midday haze fumbles over the armies, limning the jostling helmets with a kind of smoke. But you've always been a bit fond of our king, haven't you?

Yes, the red-beard nods, I have . . . ever since that eastern campaign, when Antiochus was still young . . . he'd had many defeats, faced so many rebellions, and it looked like all the satraps would pull away and his realm would disappear, but he persevered.

Our first fight together was against the Medes.

Yes, and afterward we were in the front lines in Bactria . . . at the battle of the Harīrūd.

And then, Antiochus kept us at the siege of Balkh for three years.

I grew up during those years, the red-beard says.

You mean you stopped shaving then.

There is no fighting worse than fighting in a siege . . . that aged us. Do you remember how little we ate?

Yes, and worse, how little we drank.

When I was sick, you fed me from your rations.

And you did the same for me.

We did so much digging, digging latrines, digging earthworks, digging for water.

Digging graves, too.

We buried many brave comrades.

Almost none of them died in fighting, if you remember . . . it was all hunger and disease.

It's still a soldier's death, to die at the walls of some faraway city.

I forget their faces and names.

You shouldn't.

It's amazing to me that you call them comrades, the man

with the mole says; everybody is a bastard and will steal your share of bread and soup without thinking twice.

Hungry men do hungry things.

Hungry kings do hungry things.

Well, Antiochus had the wisdom to give up, to be honest and say, "Enough is enough" . . . I respect that . . . he'd saved his kingdom from so many enemies, he put down every rebellion, and he still had the wisdom to let Balkh go.

And yet your Antiochus didn't have the wisdom to say, "Let's not piss off the Romans, let's just hold on to what we've got."

That's different, that's now . . . and he's your Antiochus, too.

For the first time in this engagement, the phalanx must step backward. The two men search the ranks in front for panicked youngsters. As one, the tail leader yells, as one. Retreating too quickly gives the enemy a greater sense of forward momentum. Fall back too slowly and the phalanx risks losing shape, the front collapsing. The trick is in bending like a branch, absorbing the pressure without breaking, before snapping back again, pushing, pushing, pushing.

Arrows rattle against their outstretched spears. They can hear the Roman chants now, the invocation of alien gods and leaders and places. The lines are compressed at the front, many forward rows clumped into the battle. The two men imagine the whittling down of the phalanx, row after row deleted, till all that remains is the last line of men, bending their shoulders into the shields, bracing for the end. But it never comes to that. Being in the back of the phalanx allows them the certainty that they can run away well before they ever have to fight.

Cheers go up to their right. A war elephant barges into the Roman brigade. Through the dust, they can make out the tenuous shape of the combat, the monumental creature with its encrustation of turrets plunging into the Roman maniple, men scattering in gray silhouette. The phalanx pushes forward, regaining ground. When the Romans finally bring down the elephant, it has thundered so far behind enemy lines that its bellows are barely audible to the two men.

They call this the turning of the tide, the red-beard says.

No, it's quite a dire stalemate . . . if it keeps going on like this, we might even have to get involved.

That would do you some good.

Do me some good . . . you know what would do me some good, a new pair of shoes and bread that's not full of grit.

You should have just stayed with your wife.

That's what she said.

I mean it . . . your home, that valley . . . what a spectacular place.

I'm glad you think about it that way.

I think about it all the time . . . how many years ago did you take me there?

It was when I was married off, so maybe five years.

The red-bearded man recalls that visit. They had been released in the early winter, with the generals unwilling to feed them through the season of peace. His own home was through the mountains, through passes already frozen shut. It made more sense to winter with his friend. When they came into the valley, he knew immediately that it was the kind of place that would be unbearable to leave. Snow dusted the terracing along the hills. A brook slipped into the green ice floes of the river. Thrushes dipped in and out of the frosted brambles, berries clutched in their beaks. They were greeted by the smell of woodsmoke and the dogs coming down the track to bark them home. He remembers leaving his boots outside the door of his friend's house, walking with bare feet over the threshold straight to the central hearth, where he would sleep, bundled like a child, for blissful weeks. The mother washed his feet and those of her son, and dressed them in thick pairs of socks. She spoke a language he could not understand, so her hospitality never felt oppressive. They would talk anyway, safe in the knowledge that affection and gratitude need no understanding. During those days, he and the man with the mole would lend their arms to whatever needed doing in the village, the chopping and thatching and hammering and sifting and trapping and skinning and curing that people must do to rebuff winter. But more time was spent conserving energy. The cow was brought inside to share the nights with them. Uncles, aunts, and cousins—it seemed the entire village consisted of uncles, aunts, and cousins—would come before the second sleep to lie around the fire and tell stories and hear the stories of the man with a mole. The red-beard supposed that his friend adorned accounts of their bravery in battle, but he actually described places beyond the valley: the towering ziggurats of long-abandoned cities, the capitals of Persia bustling with the nations of the world, rugged Gandhara, where people speak Greek from one side of their mouths and the local language from the other, the desert in between, whose inhabitants count water by the drop. When they grew tired of tales, somebody would hum a tune until everybody fell asleep. The red-beard stayed awake awhile, smiling at the snoring of these people and at the comfort that one need not be at home to feel at home.

Does your family know you can read? the red-beard asked his friend one day.

If I told them they'd expect even more from me.

How did you learn?

The man with the mole lowered a pail of snow to the ground. I ran away when I was still a boy, he said, to a city, where I learned everything I could.

It amazes me that you could leave this beautiful place.

If this was everything you knew, you'd want to leave, too.

My village was more rugged, the red-beard said, it had none of these charms . . . and to top it off, most of it was washed away during a landslide.

And yet you keep your family up in those same mountains.

That's not my choice, it's theirs.

Surely they'll live where you tell them to live.

You haven't met my wife . . . she won't be budged from her people.

Same with mine.

You have a wife?

Well, a bride . . . is it so strange that a man of my age might have a bride?

No, it's just . . . why haven't I met her?

You'll meet her at the wedding in a few days.

This is a surprise.

The man with the mole laughed. It's an even bigger surprise for me.

The bride was a cousin, slender with an intelligent face and yellow teeth. It was not normal for couples to marry in the winter, but the village used the rare occasion of the visit to tie his friend to an unmarried girl. She drank so much wine at the feast that her smile flashed purple. At the end, the groom pulled his bride by the elbow to the hayloft set up for them. The red-beard kept on drinking and singing with people whom he did not understand and who did not understand him. Afterward he lay down by the hearth, listening to his friend's mother talk to herself in her sleep. She reached out and left her fingers on his cheek. He didn't push them away.

Don't go back with me in the spring, he told his friend the next day, you should stay here.

Not a chance.

This is a place worth living in.

I've lived here.

Men get tossed around the world searching for somewhere to make their lives . . . you've had one all along.

I'm not like you, the man with the mole said, I don't want to be stuck in place.

You're a married man, you're stuck now.

I could say the same for you, couldn't I?

When I don't need the money anymore, I'll stop . . . I'll go home.

The man with the mole snorted. You have the mind of a cabbage, he said, and cabbageheads like you will always need the money.

A few weeks later, after the first thaw, they left.

The battle continues. For a moment, the men are transfixed. To the left, they see the forms of horses emerging through the dust, one after the other, flanks streaming with blood, nostrils foaming. Men slump on some of the horses, but most are riderless, saddle and harness dangling from the side.

The king—the man with the mole points—the king . . . there goes the king. They watch the king tear past them, surrounded by his silver shields, fleeing to camp.

The Romans cheer. Hold, the tail leader cries. The men stay put and push against the nervous soldiers in front of them. We do not break, the red-beard yells, Alalalalalai!

The man with the mole looks at him. We should break, he says to his friend.

The red-beard sighs. It looks better if we first try not to.

Come on, what's the point of it . . . if the bloody king has already left, surely we have license to follow.

Shut up, be a man.

Fine, but only for a bit longer.

The Romans, with typical shrewdness, rain bolts on the war elephants. These creatures are normally disciplined, used to the tumult of battle, sensible to the prodding of their mahouts. But the arrows bite down and spark rage in their hearts. In a frenzy, one runs into the neighboring phalanx. The mahout grapples with the reins in vain. He watches the terrible chaos below, men losing their bearings and running away. What remains of the phalanx is compelled to the sad task of killing their own elephant. The man with the mole and the red-bearded man stick their pikes again and again into the belly of the elephant. The creature sinks to its knees and before it gives them a chance, collapses onto them.

When a phalanx loses its shape, it is no longer a phalanx but a wild sea of shipwrecked men, clinging to flotsam, desperate for shore. The Romans surge through, hooting like jackals. The two men want nothing more than to flee, but they are trapped, pinned beneath the elephant.

Help me get up, the red-beard says.

I can't, the man with the mole says, I'm stuck.

Oh, you, too.

Can't even feel my legs.

Nor can I.

We should have run when I said so.

You're blaming me for this.

No, of course not, my friend . . . you couldn't have known that an elephant would die on top of us.

Not really a soldier's death, is it? the red-beard says.

And why would that bother me?

They laugh, only a little. The battle leaves them in its wake. Far away, Roman trumpets peal in triumph. The groans of the wounded around them grow fainter. Even if they are still alive at nightfall, birds and dogs will pick at them. The scavengers that wait in the lea of all battles will strip them of their possessions. They will be two naked men, whose bodies will soon melt and fester, merging with the sad carcass of the elephant.

The red-bearded man strains to look at his friend and reaches out to touch his cheek. He is surprised how cool the skin already feels.

The man with a mole cannot move his hands. Blood sloshes within him like wine in a jar. He tries to smile at his friend, but can only think of a time a few months ago when billeted in a Syrian town. At a shrine, his friend purchased two amulets for his young twins. He took them to the stalls of the scribes. Would you wait outside? his friend asked.

Why?

Just stay outside, will you.

He watched his friend take a stool, look back over his shoulder, cover his mouth with one hand, and whisper into the ear of the scribe. The scribe nodded and engraved each amulet. What was that? the man with the mole asked afterward.

His friend had laughed and squeezed the back of his neck. I can't tell you, his friend replied, you're too close to me to know.

THE LOSS OF MUZAFFAR

The poison hid from Muzaffar's body until his fourteenth year with the Celestinis, when it filled his arteries and flooded his aorta. Doctors said he died from a sudden failure of the heart, while Grandpère Celestini whispered of the unbearable guilt Muzaffar must have had to live with after pocketing the family sapphires, even though the Celestinis, such good people really, decided against accusing someone so stalwartly loyal to them. Others, surprised that such a lean and reticent man suffered from a heart condition, blamed the unpredictable nature of old age. But Etoile the maid, who slept in the back of the neighboring town house, suspected something else when she smelled grief in the aromas of Muzaffar's irresistible cooking.

Etoile never ate the food from Muzaffar's kitchen; few who knew of him in New York ever did. The Celestinis sheltered their extraordinary cook. His name became a rumor, his talent a legend amongst postmen and dog-walkers. Grandmère Celestini seldom shared Muzaffar with guests, anxious that one mouthful of biryani or lick of jasmine sorbet might cost her the family chef, for these were hard times, and even the proud Celestinis could not pay as much as their deeper-pocketed friends. Frequent visitors to the household, therefore, grew to understand the distinction between invitations to "High Afternoon Tea" and dinner. The latter were rare indeed, perhaps once a season, while the family held teas weekly on Thursdays at precisely 4:35 in the afternoon. Little brown-haired Leila would languorously stir the pot of ginger Darjeeling while her twin, Malcolm, with the gravity of ritual, would daub twenty-two cups each with a spoon of honey. He'd leave one cup unsweetened for Mariko the corner clairvoyant, who liked entering seven minutes late in a fog of scarves and omens.

The psychic always arrived first—punctuality was desperately out of fashion in their neighborhood. The Celestinis waited quietly for the publisher, the wine seller, and the self-referential artists, the Tibetan refugee with a meaty smile, the Jerrells, who floated back and forth from the Hudson to their Caribbean home, Alun the flutist, retired diplomats from Grandpère's working days, Leila and Malcolm's small, waddling friends from school, a journalist called Viorel, neighbors they liked and neighbors they disliked, and Cecil, who always seemed lost even when he strolled in last, carrying a bottle of brandy and reciting Persian poetry. Once all were snuggled in the red glow of the sitting room, Maman Celestini would pour the tea while Papa Celestini carted out trays of diamond-shaped egg sandwiches and loaves of pound cake he loved making himself. Everyone ate while babbling between bites and gulps about the latest openings, Malcolm's recent soccer trophy, or the Chinese diaspora in Saint Kitts. Cecil recommended a jot of brandy for everybody, but after being repeatedly rebuffed, he fell into his customary wingback chair and grumbled at a wizened and deaf man (whose suit everyone admired but whose name no one remembered, not even Grandpère) about the stench of the distant Upper East Side. The old man would grin thinly, but kept his eyes on Alun the flutist's dancing fingers. Few ever skipped Celestini teas.

Celestini "dinners," on the other hand, were known for their scarcity and overwhelming awkwardness. Whenever the family particularly felt the overdue burden of social etiquette, Papa and Maman would decide on two guests and have Muzaffar prepare a slightly larger meal than usual. He also would make the table, trace with his long fingers and favorite calligrapher's pen the names of the guests on place cards, straighten the mahogany dining chairs, light two candles, and then disappear into the kitchen to await the tinkling of Grandmère's bell. She only used the bell on these occasions, as it allowed the family to avoid calling out his name. As Muzaffar flashed in and out with platters and bowls, the children remained stonily silent throughout, though any guest could hardly fault the two. Leila drooped in her chair, choked by a dozen layers of pearls, while Malcolm's cheeks flushed the same color as his impossibly bright red bow tie. The rest of the family hurried through the meal, eyeing their guests. Her forearms wrung by glittering bangles, Grandmère sat up straight and let her hooked nose arch grimly toward the visitors. Grandpère talked little. Instead, he cast worried glances from the food to the bathroom in the foyer. Papa and Maman played the reluctant hosts, dully mouthing questions-about-the-job or indictments-of-Bush that faded quickly into a sip of wine or another nervous pause and did nothing to lighten the stifling mood of gloom. Visitors would take their leave abruptly after eating, breathing deep relieved sighs once they reached the sidewalk outside. Of course, these dinners were all choreographed to distract guests from the splendor of their meal, the incredible sensibility of Muzaffar's cooking. Such was the Celestinis' dependence on a man whom they found one winter afternoon curled on their front stoop with one palm cupped against his forehead, mumbling words they never understood.

"Aadaab arz," he had said then, each gentle syllable rolled to an incomprehensible perfection that, for days after, made Malcolm and Leila scamper about the house murmuring "aadaab arz, aadaab arz" to each other while thrusting little hands to their heads until three syllables and one motion became their eternal secret language. Grandmère had brought the man inside instantly. She had Grandpère and Papa lay his thin, long frame on a sitting room sofa, while Maman brushed the ice from his cleft chin and plump eyebrows. But as soon as Grandmère went to the kitchen to make tea, the man sprung up and followed her through the house, running his fingers along the ochre walls. Grandmère was stunned when, after a brief glance around, the man busied himself about shelves and stoves, a flurry of hands and feet, like those of a dancer missing his stage. The Celestinis crowded in front of the pantry door, watching in tremulous anticipation. He stopped suddenly, turned on one heel, approached the huddled family with four even strides, and presented a mug to Grandmère. "I am Muzaffar." His voice sounded like a quilt. It was the best cup of tea she'd ever had.

Without much of a fuss the Celestinis adopted Muzaffar, initially out of Grandmère's insistence that humanity had an obligation to protect thin people from winter, and then permanently after Muzaffar's voluntary assumption of all duties within the kitchen. Against polite protests and the furious batting of his eyelashes, the family forced a salary upon Muzaffar, a monthly wad of bills, half of which he tucked unceremoniously into the back of a kitchen drawer next to the fondue forks, and half he left caught in the springs of the cot he kept in the kitchen. Papa and Maman had felt exceedingly uncomfortable (or at least felt that they should feel exceedingly uncomfortable) at the prospect of a slender brown man toiling for nothing in their home. As Papa explained to Grandmère one evening, peering over the top of his newspaper, the money justified the man's role in the house. How else could they explain his most bizarre presence?

Though Grandmère accepted her son's clipped reasoning,

she had guiltily entertained fantasies of a man so warm and generous that he would appreciate welcome and shelter with a passion for kitchen work, that relationships need never make economic sense as long as they were dimly poetic. His reluctant acquiescence to a wage cast Muzaffar as her romantically tragic (or even tragically romantic) hero. This veiled dreaminess of Grandmère's, uncharacteristic for a lady who woke up every morning to ensure that the baggy-eyed Sanitation Department truck picked up all the garbage in front of their stoop, had already infected the entire family. It seemed that Muzaffar's arrival tickled the Celestinis out of character. In the first weeks, Grandpère began to return from his daily dusk strolls with pots of petunias, which he had Leila and Malcolm balance on the many crumbling windowsills so that pink petals fluttered against the gray face of the house. Grandpère hoped the effect would make their home look like Florence, lavender memories glimmering again in his eyes. Maman dragged the children into the kitchen, where, to Muzaffar's great bemusement, the three Celestinis proceeded to make guava jelly from a faded family recipe. "Our generation doesn't make jam anymore!" she berated Papa the next morning. Papa, too consumed by his own fantasies to care for confectionery, spent day and night rearranging and dusting the family's hoard of books. At least two rooms in each of the town house's three floors boasted floor-to-ceiling, wall-to-wall bookshelving, all of which suffered from a severe case of accumulated disorder. He decided to set things straight, whizzing zealously about with a plumed duster and knowledge of the Dewey Decimal System. Suddenly, the poems of Mahmoud Darwish no longer found themselves beside Herodotus, Calvino extracted himself from Sun Tzu, Walcott escaped the clutches of Durkheim. Papa even found the fake book in which Grandpère had intended to stow the Celestini family sapphires but had instead left adrift alongside Brecht (snatching the fake book from her son and glaring at her bemused husband, Grandmère placed the jewels inside the book's hollow and slipped it innocuously into her study). After twenty-one days, Papa became hopeful. Perhaps if he could order the incomparable insanity of the Celestini bookshelves, reason would even return to the warring world. Humanity, after all, was nothing but a library. Papa finished his work a month later, happily optimistic and blissfully unaware that Malcolm and Leila had switched books around in his wake, sowing the seeds of a new chaos in unknowable whispers, "aadaab arz, aadaab arz."

Muzaffar was absorbed by the Celestini household through these abrupt impulses, through a family epidemic of mischievous inspiration, and, above all, through the unrivaled superiority of his cooking. Breakfast, packed food for the children's meals at school, lunch, a light tea for Grandpère and Maman, and dinner. The cycle repeated itself daily, Muzaffar's tireless work pausing only on Thursdays in the afternoon, and sometimes when it had snowed lightly and slush had yet to fill the gutters. The elder Celestinis insisted he take more breaks, even offered to pay him for time off, but he shrugged them away with a delicate smile and an even more delicate mango mousse. How could the Celestinis complain? Malcolm and Leila never lacked friends throughout elementary school, middle school, and even high school. Students crowded about them during lunch period, hoping for a nibble of sun-dried tomato ravioli or finely spiced merguez. In college, many a steamy night for both Celestini brother and sister began with a dark chocolate torte or several portobello pancakes in a mint sauce, which always arrived at their dorms neatly wrapped in white packaging and including a card that, in elegant letters, read "Aadaab Arz." Grandmère and Grandpère also benefited from Muzaffar's food. Despite their steadily advancing age, they never contracted arthritis, hemorrhoids, bladder irregularities, Alzheimer's, cancer, or even the common cold, though Grandpère still occasionally developed cases of gout—that, he blamed on his ancestors. Like both grandparents, Papa and Maman thrived off their cook; during Muzaffar's fourteen-year tenure, none of the Celestini adults felt any older. Time thickened and settled about the house like beaten cream in a soufflé.

Muzaffar, too, didn't grow older. Only his eyebrows evidenced the passage of time. They billowed and turned a quiet silver, two lost rain clouds above the doldrums of his eyes. This graying struck the family as particularly odd, since Muzaffar seemed altogether outside the bounds of history. Each of the Celestinis soon realized that it was pointless inquiring about him. If asked about the land of his birth, or his age, Muzaffar would laugh and later emerge at dinner with a grilled swordfish and declare, "This is where I'm from!" or, after placing a goat cheese tart on the table, clap once: "That, my dears, is the sum of my years." Likewise, he explained his ethnicity with a chestnut soup, while his childhood was one of eggplants and quails. His family consisted of twenty-four cupcakes; he elaborated his political beliefs in dumplings; and the path that had finally brought him to the Celestinis' stoop appeared in the burnt trails of roasted tomatoes. Grandmère suspected Muzaffar hid himself in his food so that the Celestinis would digest bits of him every day, only ever knowing the man by his endless flavors. It seemed, to her, a wonderfully appropriate game for their sublime cook to play.

In this way, the Celestinis never saw Muzaffar outside his talent. But he was not what he cooked, or at least, not entirely what he cooked. Every Thursday afternoon, as the Tibetan refugee sung from his throat or Viorel took black-and-white photographs of Leila and her little friends with their jaws set and fists in the air, Muzaffar drifted about the city. When the sun was out, he'd join pickup soccer games in the park at St. Luke's Place. During every World Cup, these games grew in length and intensity, spilling into the streets after the park closed at dusk. Muzaffar was always the referee. Other Thursdays, he went east to Ludlow Street, where he joined an old Cantonese lady whose earlobes brushed against her shoulders and whose eyes were as still as his. She sat cross-legged on a bench blowing smoke rings from a thin water pipe. He liked letting the smoke out in slow thick streams through his nostrils and would sit there, watching buses and taxis blur until the coals died out. When it rained and only soggy black shapes slunk through the streets, Muzaffar ran alongside Alphabet City boys as they sprayed "East Side" on unsuspecting West Village town houses—but he always did steer the boys away from the Celestinis'. No one in the house knew of their cook's wanderings, none thought Muzaffar capable of anything else. So it was that whenever he traced his way back to his adopted home, past Mariko's ramshackle stall, through the misty lamplight of Commerce Street till he reached the old stoop and the pink-flowered gray town house, Muzaffar belonged to New York City, not the Celestini kitchen. Etoile the Haitian maid watched him from the ground-floor window of the neighboring town house, watched as he paused before mounting the Celestini stoop, watched in winter as he skimmed ice from the wrought-iron railings with a slender forefinger. Perhaps it was understanding that drew her eyes. She, too, belonged to New York City—more than she did to pots and pans and red-cheeked babies, a vacuum cleaner, or even to the divine smells of Muzaffar's cooking that spread through the walls of town houses and into her daydreams.

Once they strolled together to the shore of the Hudson, where arm in arm (Etoile was always charmed by Muzaffar's gallantry) they walked south toward the World Trade Center. She told him about her families, the one here that she coddled, the one there that she missed. He made her watch the seagulls fuss about the stumps of a long-vanished pier. The sun set behind New Jersey, turning the cold river orange. A clutter of yachts bobbed against their moorings. In the wind and spray of the water, they could barely hear the city pulsing behind them. They felt alone, as if the city were but a backdrop for their meandering, a vista built for them. Just imagine, Muzaffar said, looking over the river, just imagine how many people have come here through the years, the centuries, to make this place their own.

She was imagining that on the infamous day New York lost its towers, the day ash fell like snow across the neighborhood, the day Mariko forgave the future and closed her shop, the day before Muzaffar's last. Fire trucks and ambulances zoomed through the catatonic streets, chasing billowing black clouds. Schools emptied. Hulking office buildings ground to a halt. Lower Manhattan stayed eerily silent, gagged by yellow caution tape and the soot-laden air. The Cantonese lady abandoned her bench, earlobes swinging behind her as she fled to Flushing. Soccer balls lay strewn about St. Luke's Place like the toys of ghosts. Somewhere, giants began to play with the television and wrinkled white men, staring grimly toward Heaven, decided the fate of language. It seemed to Etoile, beside the ground-floor window, that the neighborhood, the entire city even, was sinking into an alien world of ash, interminably gray and powerfully lonely. She fumbled with the nozzle of her vacuum cleaner, longing to suck away all the soot, longing to return color to her Commerce Street. But in the upstairs playroom, the babies broke into a wail and drew Etoile from her grounded flights of fancy.

In his kitchen, Muzaffar abandoned a promising lunch and slipped like a shadow through the Celestini house. He had made a decision. Expressionless except for his stormy eyebrows, Muzaffar stole into Grandmère's study, found that book he knew to be a fake, and from its hollow removed the Celestini sapphires, sneaking the storied heirlooms into the pocket of his apron.

The jewels had been taken before. They were first stolen almost two hundred years ago, on the green island of Ceylon, where colonial officers made men slither through the mines in search of stones more precious than their lives. A grizzled jewel-cutter, his eyes turning to milk, slid the sapphires into his underwear and descended from the mountains, through a forest of eucalyptus trees, and came to the port. He sold the stones to a sea captain for enough money to soften a long, jagged life under empire. Tucked within a crate of tea, the sapphires sailed past the hills of Aden, into the bustle and dust of Zanzibar, and round the nose of Africa till they reached the Canaries, when pirates set upon the ship and stripped it of all its cargo. Craving the gleam of Malay pearl, or Indian silver, or even Chinese oranges, the pirates found only crate after crate of tea, which they sold in disgust to a distributor in Cádiz. The sapphires soon crossed through the Pyrenees, looped around Marseille, and tumbled through the Tuscan countryside to Florence, where they emerged quite unexpectedly in Elio Celestini's morning cup of tea. He jumped from the veranda of the villa, yelling for a larder girl, who, with a quivering hand, pointed out the recently purchased package of Ceylon tea leaves. Years later, Elio would tell his children of how, by God's infinite grace, the Celestini family had been given jewels as blue and true as their eyes, and that, as long as the sapphires stayed within the family, the Celestinis would be content and have no secrets to keep, and would never forget their history. The sapphires lingered in Florence, leaving in Grandpère's breast pocket more than a century later when he escaped decline and faded grandeur for Paris and the warm arms of Grandmère. They rented a walk-up in the Marais, and together learned how to dance and how to think. In those days, the sapphires glimmered and spun within the bowels of Grandmère's record player. But, restless again, the Celestini jewels followed the family to the gray town house on Commerce Street, where they could shelve all their books and put their sapphires finally to rest.

Muzaffar waited a day before taking the sapphires out of his apron. By then, Grandpère had already opened the empty book and found them missing. The Celestinis had skittered about the house, going through the motions of a search for something that could never just be lost, unwilling for the first time in fourteen years to bring themselves to the table and eat. It was only a matter of hours before eyes turned on the cook, sapphire eyes crying both for their broken New York City and for their suddenly missing past. Grandmère's nose bent viciously as Muzaffar removed the platter of tangerine couscous from the table. "How can you think of food at a time like this?" she hissed. "Is it all you care about?" He said nothing but glided back and forth from the kitchen, untouched dishes in hand, while Grandpère muttered black thoughts in the dark of the foyer bathroom. Maman collapsed in the sitting room, feeding herself spoonful after spoonful of guava jelly as Papa, unable to reach the twins at their dorms, let the television wash over his numb eyes.

Alone in the kitchen, Muzaffar poured the sapphires out onto the countertop. The jewels were each no larger than his thumbnail, uncertain teardrops under the pale kitchen light. He scooped them all into one cupped hand, and with a flick of his wrist, dropped them into an already sizzling pan. Amid onions, red peppers, streams of puréed tomatoes, powdered turmeric, cloves, and a mound of chopped okra, the sapphires tossed and fried. In all their travels, they had never encountered the fervor of a cook possessed, the heat of a man breaking from his adopted home. Muzaffar's eyebrows twitched with each shake of the pan. He stirred relentlessly, so frantic in his movements that even his eternally still eyes swirled, catching the blue, now brown, now green light of sapphires disappearing into a stir-fry. Then he stopped, apparently satisfied with the thick smell of burnt okra clouding the kitchen. There would be time, later, he knew, for families to eat and forget, to float uninvited from place to place, to speak words no one understood, to love the city with their eyes, even to be a New Yorker and serve nothing, but not now. Not when colors had fled the world and left maids alone, clinging to unspoken odors. With serene and slow bites, he finished the entire pan, and waited for the poison of the Celestinis to spread and preserve lost history in the memory of his food.

THE ASTROLABE

In the spring of 1422, a squadron of two-masted galleys sailed west from Tunis. Past Gibraltar, the Atlantic spread before them, green and cold-blooded, hissing with the threat of serpents. They turned south, shadowing the land, rowing against the wind. Their goal was to round Bojador, the long arm of sand and rock at the end of the known world, beyond which few sailors had ever gone. All seamen told stories about Bojador. There, the water boiled in sudden whirlpools. Those ships that managed to skirt the whirlpools were wrapped in steam and dragged invariably to a bigger drop, the biggest of them all, where the world ocean fell off its even plane and tumbled into space.

The captain of the squadron was a zealous man who had no patience for the bilge-speak of sailors. He believed that it was possible to weather the winds and make the tip of Bojador, that the world didn't end there or the sea give way, but that the coast bent back into the continent, arcing east to hotter climes full of gold and salt and slaves. His drummers beat a stern pace. The sails held tight in the rigging and the wind poured through the gunwales. He spoke to his subordinates in intervals, since all talk was drowned by the great creaking rhythm of the oars.

They never got close to Bojador. A storm fulminated out of the south. Too late, the captain signaled his ships to turn for the safety of a harbor. The galleys were hurled toward shore, shattering against hidden reefs. He wrenched his own ship the other way, but a sail blew free and the lateen yawned taut with merciless air. The storm drove them out into the ocean.

Oars splintered, scything whole rows of men at the torso. Others washed overboard. In flashes of lightning, sailors on the rigging thought they saw monsters chomping in the foam. The captain lashed himself to the crumbling deck. All night, his ship dipped under waves, heaving into the air and through spray to the dizzying point that he felt his mind lift away from body and beam. A lightness filled the hollow timbers. It seemed that his ship was gliding onward in a flat line, as if the storming sea and sky were paper cutouts with all the reality of shadow puppetry.

He experienced the rest of his shipwreck like he was watching a puppet show. An island entered in the foreground and his ship, tiring of its role, soared head-on into collision. Flailing marionettes, his men sank below the rim of the stage. Fragments of the wreck pulled back out to sea and tossed around further islands. The captain saw himself holding on to debris, blowing and sucking like a fish, the gelatinous bulk of the ocean throbbing beneath.

The storm slackened. Alone, he edged toward a dark shore. These must be the Fortunate Isles, he recalled, once a continent in its own right according to the Greeks (but what do they know), now only a bunch of mountainous islands inhabited by idol-worshipping savages . . . They are the westernmost people in the world, famous for their ignorance, the muscular sex of their women, and the indigo dye you can harvest from a mollusk that washes up on their beaches. The captain's recitation came partly in cold words, partly in syllables of seawater, but it calmed him. He felt like Sindbad, condemned to soliloquize on driftwood. What would the restless mariner have done in situations like this? Opportunist that he was, Sindbad would have prayed. So the captain began to mumble his prayers, which turned like so many into a lament: Oh God, I, your lickspittle servant, have done nothing to deserve this doom so please find it within your infinite grace to give me a break. The curtains closed, darkness fell upon the stage, and the captain swooned into unconsciousness.

He dreamt of falling through the water. Assemblies of fish drifted by, then a divan of squids, and great religious processions of whales carrying the bones and beards of their saints. Clouds of dust rose from the deep and soon he could see nothing at all, but kept on sinking, the dust filling his nose and mouth. With a bump, he landed on something hard. Something hit him in the chest. He struggled to see. The object hit him again and he held on to it, slick and dense. He was pulled forward and then backward. It was the shaft of an oar. He found himself seated on the bench of a galley, surrounded by his drowned sailors, all heaving in concert as they stirred the dust of the ocean floor.

The captain awoke on the beach practically naked, his clothes shredded by the storm. He tore off the rags to bind wounds on his arms and legs. Slowly, he lifted himself to his feet. The world wobbled before coming into focus. It was a narrow beach, giving way to a forest that lapped in laurel thickness up the side of a mountain. The sky was a quiet blue. Peeking above a high ridge, the sun rubbed his nudity with light. He saw no sign of other people.

God is hearing, God is seeing . . . whoever desires the reward of the world, then with God is its reward. The captain sank to his knees in prayer, giving thanks to the creator, angels, all the spirits that buoyed him from death, even the sharks for sparing his sad flesh. Renewed, he strode into the world. The talk of finches guided him to fresh water. Like a puff of steam, a firecrest appeared on his shoulder. You are a bird, he said. He cupped the creature in his hands, gently, as if it were the first of its kind. He named the insects, the moss, the dervish arms of trees. He climbed higher. Pastures rolled above the forest, speckled here and there with grazing animals. You are a goat, he said as he chased a goat, you were made in the image of man's need. Wrestling the creature to the ground, he put his mouth to its udders and began to suck the milk.

The goatherds came then. What on earth are you doing? they said, but the captain didn't understand, and in any case his mouth was overflowing with milk. The goatherds clouted him over the head. They bundled him up and took him to their village.

The villagers turned out to inspect him. It seemed to the captain, as he shook himself upright, that the natives were a people of the goat. They wore goat-skin robes and jackets. They smelled of mutton. Some of them had slicked their brown hair with animal fat. Their faces were narrow and pinched, but their lips and noses had a bluntness that gave them an obstinate, slightly glum look. He was taller than the tallest of them, so he stood, indifferent to his nakedness, and spoke. I am a captain of Tunis, a man of means and good repute, and I'd be grateful if you kind people would do me the honor of your hospitality . . . some food, some drink, some clothing, and if you don't mind, a bed for me to rest.

They stared at him, uncomprehending. The crowd shifted to allow the approach of a gray-haired woman. She handed a cloth to the captain to cover himself and motioned for him to sit down. Her robe was so long that it covered her feet. She lowered herself next to him and took his hand in hers. He was startled by her touch. Do any of you understand Arabic? he asked. She looked at him mutely. How about Greek? My Greek is not bad, you see . . . Sunday, Monday, Tuesday, Wednesday . . . leeward, windward, riptide, current . . . Scorpio, Libra, Pisces. The woman turned his hand over and inspected his fingers. From the back of the crowd, somebody whistled. From the captain's left came another whistle. The whole village shook with laughter, including the woman, revealing her little pointed teeth.

My god, the captain thought, this is a nightmare from the tales of Sindbad . . . I've come to an island of tongueless cannibals.

He tried again, ransacking his sailor's locker for all the words he'd collected on the sea. You might understand some Castilian, he said, and spouted a few phrases. Majorcan maybe? Genoese? Please, you people must understand something, it's not as if you live that far away . . . Don't tell me you're Jews. Berber? Sardinian? Portuguese? How about French?

Yes, the gray-haired woman said, I understand French-speak. Oh, French. French, yes. She smiled at him. Good, good, the captain said in French and then looked in defeat at his lap. It occurred to him that his own French was rather meager and picked up in brothels. Who are you? she asked. I am a captain of Tunis. What is Tunis? Tunis big town far away, many ships. Why are you here and not in Tunis? My ship break. Where is your ship? Tell me, where am I, what island this, this France? Where is your ship? My ship break, no more erect. The captain mimed its disintegration with his hands, one hand arching like a wave, the other cupped like the foundering boat. Where are your men? The woman squeezed his knee. The captain shrugged. No more men. His hands motioned the sinking of bodies beneath the sea. Surprising himself, he began to weep.

She put an arm around his shoulders. What is inside this? The gray-haired woman pointed to the pouch that he wore around his neck. Show it to me, she said.

In normal circumstances, the captain would never let others touch his most valuable possessions. He felt he had no choice but to undo the thong and hand over the pouch. She slid the contents onto the ground: his father's coral ring, a small book of prayer, a charm against the evil eye, and most conspicuous of all, his astrolabe.

The villagers pressed in close to inspect the astrolabe, its moving brass plates and intricate lines. You eat your food from this, the gray-haired woman said. No, no. The captain didn't know the word in French, so he translated from Arabic: This takes the stars. The gray-haired woman translated what he had said into her own language and the villagers murmured and smiled, looking at him with a kind of pity. They thought him touched. You pray to this then? It is your god? There is no god but God and Muhammad is his messenger, the captain said in Arabic. Then he spat in French, pointing up to the sky. My god is not a thing, he is one god. The gray-haired woman nodded knowingly. Of course, we have that kind of god, too.

She ran her fingers over the various markings of the astrolabe. Your god's plate is very beautiful, she said, what does it tell you?

The captain inhaled. Long ago, he had a better grasp of the logic behind the astrolabe, but that knowledge had silted into his mind and lost its definition. He knew simply to trust the astrolabe's measurements. The prospect of having to relate its functions in his whorehouse French exhausted him. How could he explain such grand concepts with so few words? How could he make them understand that the astrolabe represented the flattened sphere of the universe, that mathematical principles undergirded the wonder and ephemera of the world, that land, water, and sky were divisible in degrees, that the earth was rung with lines of latitude just as the heavens fell into their own grid, that a ship on the sea plots its terrestrial address in a landscape of stars? Please, he said, some drink and food. A plate was brought to him of polenta and unsalted cheese. The gray-haired woman poured liquid from a goat-skin into his mouth. It tasted enough like wine.

This takes the stars, the captain began, also other things. You use it to tell time . . . you can use it to see how high things are . . . you use it to see the planets dance. What do you mean, tell time? I mean the time of day . . . so I know when to pray. Can't you look at the sun? It's not so easy. Don't you know how high things are? Do you . . . Tell me, how tall is that mountain? That mountain is as tall as that mountain. That isn't a size. Show us something then, make your god work.

The captain rose with the astrolabe. I need a hand. This one helps, the gray-haired woman said, and pushed a young girl toward the captain. Tell her to look through here . . . keep still . . . when she sees top, tell me. The girl did as she was instructed, angling the astrolabe to the point that it aligned with the mountain peak. She grunted. The captain took the reading in degrees. There, you see, mountain is this high . . . now you can see if mountain is taller or shorter than other mountains.

The gray-haired woman shrugged. We only have one mountain . . . anyway, I'll tell you how high it is . . . it takes a healthy young woman two days of climbing to reach the very top . . . I did that once . . . now, why don't you show me how the planets dance?

It was possible to make celestial readings with his astrolabe, but that required adjusting for the object's home latitude, which in the case of this device was forty degrees for Tunis, the city where his astrolabe was made. He would first have to determine his current latitude and then adjust the celestial readings on the tympanum for his present location. The process was beyond him. I'm too soft, the captain said, I can't do it. That is a shame, can we help you? The captain shook his head.

The gray-haired woman might have described to the captain

their own system of astrology, the way her people aligned the openings of their tombs with the rays of the spring sun, how they read shapes not only in the spider webs of the stars but in the purple darkness in between, a cartography of black rivers in the sky, how some of their neighbors tracked the movement of the female planets, others the male, how on clear summer nights they all went to the high spots to enumerate the stars and the shadows of stars. But she, too, was growing tired of speaking this language that was neither hers nor his.

You want to know how I can talk French-speak? Okay, how do you know French-speak? the captain asked. They made me learn it. Who? The French. In France? No, they came here many years ago. This is not France? No . . . they tried to rule us for a while and give us their god . . . when I was young I was taken as a servant . . . they were very hard on me. I'm sorry. No matter, we killed them all in the end. Oh.

The rheum stirred in her eyes and the captain sensed her voice taking on a cold steel. Your men, she said, all gone? I think so. Only you left? Yes, only me. Nobody else? Nobody, only me. She sighed and rose stiffly to her feet. In her own language, she summoned the young girl, who gathered up the captain's things. Before the captain could protest, the girl fled back into the crowd. Bodies closed in around him. They hoisted him over their heads and carried him higher, out of the village and up onto a climbing path. Rough hands reached through the thicket of flesh to daub his body in fat. The captain thrashed and yelled, but the hands that held him were implacable.

He grew still. By the time they hurled him from the cliff, he had surrendered. *No people can hasten their fate, nor postpone it.* The captain fell without a cry. Air screamed between his eyelashes and it seemed as if the clouds had taken the shapes of whales. *There is nothing but our life of this world, and we shall not be raised*. The villagers watched the waves take his broken body from the rocks into the sea.

The gray-haired woman returned to her dark home. She emptied the captain's pouch onto her bed. The astrolabe gleamed with russet magic in the firelight. She let her fingers trace its many grooves, its curving designs, the spiraling letters. The French, too, had their ways of writing. It seemed all the outsiders did. The young girl was in the corner watching. She'd been waiting for her. I know you're feeling bad, the girl said. I don't like having to make these decisions . . . it is hard. Don't feel bad, grandmother, it's better this way. We could have kept him with us, made him one of us. No, that is impossible. How do you know? She turned to the youngster. How do you know, little one? She admired the girl's stillness, her unmoving gaze. When he fell, the girl said, he did not fall like a man or a chicken or a dog, he fell like a stone.

ICEBREAKERS

It takes only moments for an icebreaker in the Antarctic to come to the profound realization that it can no longer break ice. The Russian ship carries sailors, engineers, a cook, a doctor, a communications officer, a team of researchers, a handful of journalists, a photographer, and an asthmatic captain. When the boat shudders and stops, they zip up their red bubble coats and crowd the railings. We're stuck, we're stuck, we're stuck. Word spreads around the ship. The captain wheezes the command to reverse, but to no avail. The icebreaker is hemmed in. We're stuck, we're stuck, we're stuck, cry the throng of sailors at the rear. The engineers report back, shaking their heads. The captain fumbles for his inhaler. If an icebreaker can't break ice, what can?

A bigger icebreaker, of course. They radio for rescue, the communications officer paddling the distress signal. In the modern world, there is always somebody within reach. A Chinese boat responds quickly: Stay put, comrades, we're coming for you.

To kill time, the crew scatters about the ice. The cook sets up a cauldron of hot chocolate. Staring across the rough white vastness, the journalists struggle with their metaphors. The photographer wishes for just a few penguins.

The researchers take samples and measurements. We know that the glaciers of the continent are shrinking, they tell the captain, but nobody understands the growth of the sea ice around Antarctica. Every year, the crust on the cold ocean swells. The dizzying labor of NASA satellites has not helped explain why. It could be caused by precipitation, changing atmospheric conditions, a general cooling in the regional water, expansionist molecules, who knows. Sea ice is as mysterious as it is dangerous. Gusts of westerly air blow its piratical floes into sudden hedges, into walls so thick a free-moving twelve-thousand-ton icebreaker finds its passage blocked on all sides. Strictly speaking, they say, our ship's predicament is not the fault of the ice but the conspiracy of the wind.

At night, the crew return to the ice-locked ship, where they drink vodka and argue over which movie to screen in the little auditorium. There's no consensus. They veto an Eisenstein epic as too nationalist and too smothered in ice. (This isn't the time to watch people drown in freezing water, even Germans.) They reject a Hollywood disaster movie as uncomfortably near their own situation. In the end, the engineers and sailors have their way. The crew spend the rest of the evening watching a Bollywood film, one typically long enough to put everybody to sleep. Most of them have already dribbled off to their bunks by the time the film reaches its happy climax. The hero and heroine, bundled in earmuffs and scarves, dance around an alpine mountain and make angels in the snow.

The photographer dutifully captures the scene: the nearly empty auditorium, one sailor slumped asleep in his chair, the Indian heartthrobs flickering on-screen. She imagines a magazine feature, or an Internet click-through, or even a narrated slideshow, her own gravelly voice captioning the curious ordeal. She works around the ship, snapping away. In the galley, the cook already sweats over the morning porridge—breakfast times come quickly in the polar summer. He grins at her and poses with his ladle, outstretched and dripping. Engineers on the late shift peer at gauges in the boiler room. They thumbs-up and say in faltering English, Ship machines are A-OK. Some of the researchers and journalists are awake playing cards in the rec room. Why is it, one of them asks as she takes their profiles, that Russians love Indian films so much? I'm Indian and I can't bloody watch them for a second.

She crests the rattling interior passageways and box-like compartments, emerging out into the cold. The boat has been anchored in place so the floes won't shepherd it to an even worse fate. Frost chaps the railings and slicks the deck. The blue murmur of morning spreads on the horizon. Up above, she sees a glimmer in the bridge and the hunched form of the captain. She takes a few shots from a distance, then climbs up to him, knocks on the open door. You wouldn't mind if I took your close-up? she asks. The captain rises, sweater billowing about his narrow frame, and closes the door. He feels the ice closing in around his ship and struggles for breath.

Two days later, the Chinese ship appears on the horizon. Please free us soon, the communications officer tells them, I'm sick of watching Indian movies.

Okay, the Chinese captain says, make your infirm and nonessential crew line up single file by the side of the ship . . . we'll land our helicopter on the ice and begin evacuating the lot of them.

The Russian captain takes the radio from the communications officer. Thank you, he says, I'll make sure my crew are disembarked safely, I'll keep my watch. He speaks in thin breaths and all that the Chinese hear on their end is vapor, a crackle, the possibility of speech.

The engineers find the flattest bank of ice near the ship. They trace the markings of a helipad with red spray paint, much to the delight of the photographer, who captures this fragile conquest of ice. The helicopter thunders into view. Everybody waves as it lands, glad to be buffeted by its gale. The pilot hops out, shaking his head. Bad news, he tells the communications officer, I just got word from the bridge . . . it seems our boat is stuck, too.

The best use of the helicopter that day is in a process of useful exchange, bringing DVDs and crates of vodka one way and food the other. Many of the crew on the Chinese ship are Filipinos—the Ishmaels of our time—including, thankfully, their cook. On the Russian vessel, they now feast on chicken and rice porridge, steamed *lumpia* filled with minced coconut and pork, and adobo lamb stewed in lemongrass. After gorging himself, the Russian cook returns to his galley and stares at his cleavers and paring knives. Of what worth are his skills with potatoes and beets when compared with the genius of the calamansi?

The captain of the Russian icebreaker flies over to consult his counterpart. He admires the Chinese ship's state of good repair, its clean orange lines, the state-of-the-art medical facilities, the pleasing girth of its hull and its red-cheeked crew. In the captain's quarters he sips vodka, holding it in his mouth and letting it trickle down his throat, as if that slow fire could spread to his lungs. We are fifteen kilometers from you, the Chinese captain says, and by our latest estimate, a further fifteen from more brittle, navigable ice. We're trapped like you, helpless like you, and all we can do is wait.

Well, at least you have the helicopter, the Russian captain says. They speak in English, which is the language of the sea, of the air, and of space, even if it will never fully conquer the land.

Yes, and the helicopter is as useful as two tin cans tied by string. They laugh. Neither of them has ever held tin cans tied by string.

I've been told that the Australians are sending a boat to help us. I must confess, I'm embarrassed.

Me too. We've given the Aussies a chance to feel generous.

I'm sorry to have dragged you into this mess.

We can't know the whims of the ice. I never imagined that this could happen, that all this steel of mine could be defeated.

It may be easier for the evacuation to the Aussie ship if I transfer most of my people to you.

It will be. We are ready when you are.

And please thank your cook. If the reports I'm hearing are true, he's putting our own man out of a job.

The Chinese captain leans over and puts a hand on the Russian's knee. Forgive me, but I must say . . . are you quite well? You look really dreadful.

Do I? The Russian captain startles. It is easy to spend days on a ship without glancing at a mirror, and he has not made much of an effort to keep up appearances. It's the asthma, he says, sometimes it can't take this cold.

Let me ask my doctor to have a look at you.

No, no, that's all right, nothing to worry about, the captain insists, I have my own man . . . but thank you, that's very kind. The captain treasures these gestures, these courtesies of life at sea, all their generosity and camaraderie, reminders that in the marine, man returns to his natural state of friendship and love for man. He leaves his counterpart with a rigid bow, a movement he thinks appropriate for the occasion. The Chinese captain responds in kind. Neither of them has bowed like that before. On the helicopter back to his own ship, the captain sits in the midst of steaming containers of *lechon*, roast pork stuffed with star anise and spring onion. He searches for breaks in the sea ice below, but finds none.

When he lands, the communications officer receives him

with a full update. The crew has begun boiling snow to conserve water reserves—at sea, nothing is as precious as water. The engineers plan to power down nonessential sections of the ship, though they promise to keep the auditorium open for screenings. The researchers have taken the four-wheelers for a spin on the ice. Our cook seems depressed, so he's been tasked with making cocktails for the journalists, who—no matter where they are—think it's their professional privilege to be drunk.

As feared, the ice is still too thick near the ship to allow any progress. The captain breathes deeply from his inhaler. I should have known better, he thinks. Misled by weather forecasts and satellite imagery, he let his boat venture deep into the sea ice. Often, polar winds keep channels of water free, passages that Arctic and Antarctic sailors call polynyas (Russian is the language of ice). The captain steered his expedition down a known polynya, only to find it close around him. Greater dangers lie in the ice floes than scarcity and loneliness. Sea currents threaten to shear icebergs toward his pinned ship. That is the strange irony of their position; the ship is stuck, moored in place, even as the thick ice around it continues to move. The captain looks out from the bridge in the grim twilight, katabatic clouds of crystals blowing down from the glaciers, ice stretching in its infinity to meet another horizon of ice, while somewhere beneath roam the silent trunks of icebergs, blue and rootless.

Tomorrow, he tells the communications officer, we'll begin evacuating our passengers to the Chinese ship.

When the sun sets, the Australian icebreaker is still several hundred kilometers away. Few of the crew on either ship have the willpower to stay awake. Like peasants in millennia of winters, they curl up in their bunks for long sleeps. The captain stays up on the bridge, poring over charts and the latest satellite imagery. The photographer also slips about. She relishes the soft rust glow of the ship's lamps, the sky's cushion of dark.

The two of them stop their work to look at the aurora. It snakes across the horizon the whole night (all three hours of it), green bands thickening in ribbons and waves, shivering in ripples of purple, before it exhausts its cosmic breath and wraps the ice in a fiery fuzz. The photographer captures it all and goes to bed at dawn triumphant. The captain hears noise in the aurora, a swishing and a snap, like the crack of linens hung out to air. In the Antarctic, the silence is so total that even light carries sound.

The next morning, as the researchers gather their things and head to the waiting Chinese helicopter, they assure the captain that the aurora australis is entirely inaudible to the human ear. What he heard was an illusion, the leakage of electrical matter from his eye into those regions of the brain responsible for sound. The captain shakes his head, incredulous, imagining the storm behind his eyes, lightning seeping into the pink stuff. It was more physical than that, he says, as if something popped beneath my skin.

The researchers shrug. Nothing in the world, they say, is as wondrous as the human mind. They hug the crew and the captain. Later in the day, the helicopter extracts the journalists swaddled in their snow coats, rubbing their noses and burping.

As soon as he is left with his permanent crew, the captain visits his doctor. Tell me, he says in Russian (it is a relief to speak in one's own language), tell me why I'm having such trouble breathing. Is it my asthma?

The doctor prods him with his stethoscope. Deep breaths, please, he says. He looks at the instrument, slaps it against his palm, then returns it to the captain's back. I hear static, he says.

Static? Eh? What kind of doctor are you?

No need to be accusatory.

Not a wheeze?

You're crackling.

What's that supposed to mean?

That I need to move you to the Chinese ship for proper diagnosis. And that you shouldn't exert yourself at all.

Nothing doing. You know full well I have a responsibility to this ship.

Don't try to play the hero.

It's that bad, is it.

It could be.

The captain slumps in his chair. I'm no hero, he says, peering up at the doctor with his eyes watering, the tattoos on his pale chest stretched and loose.

As the captain is strapped into the helicopter for the last evacuation of the day, the communications officer leans into his ear with news that the Australian icebreaker is stuck fast, surrounded by impenetrable sea ice. I knew it, the captain says flatly, I felt it happen inside me.

On board the Chinese icebreaker, the journalists are already busy making names for themselves, e-mailing in their stories from the ship's computer lab. Their plight has become the stuff of international headlines, gifted various Twitter hashtags, Photoshopped into stills of the TV show *Game of Thrones* (blue-eyed zombies surround the boats), even mined for clicks in lists like "16 Sexiest Captains to Be Trapped with in the Antarctic" and "Top 10 Most Edible & Expendable Antarctic Expedition Professions" ("#1 Journalists," "#10 Mechanics"), the implication being that the crew of the three stranded ships are now only a few missed meals away from cannibalism.

Nothing could be further from the truth. The researchers crowd the galley, feasting on the miracles of its Filipino chef: noodles steeped in orange shrimp broth, oxtail stew with banana blossoms and peanuts, papaya-stuffed empanadas. They are quietly ashamed that of everyone mired in this situation, they have the most reasons to be pleased. The new global attention on the Antarctic will make it much easier to secure funding for future expeditions. When no one else is looking, they clink their little glasses together and take secret shots of vodka.

As the sun rises, the photographer selects her most powerful lens and climbs to the highest spot on the Chinese ship. To the north lies the Australian boat, to the south the Russian. She studies their black, now gold silhouettes. They seem disjointed, composed from random blocks, rising from the ice desert like the ruins of lost civilizations. When the sun becomes too strong, she packs her camera away and joins the journalists for a drink.

Before the Russian captain enters the scanner, he is visited by his Chinese and Australian counterparts. They pat him on the shoulder and squeeze his hand. Did you hear, the Australian says, a little French boat coming from the west just tried to help us . . . it took one look at the ice and turned away.

They laugh, but the Russian captain can only rattle his mirth.

Many other icebreakers are on their way, the Chinese says, the world wants us all saved . . . that includes you.

The Russian captain thanks them with an apology. I should never have gone this deep, he says, the words coming out so slowly that only minutes later, when alone and under the hum of the machine, does he finish speaking.

The aurora australis returns that night, a dancing green. The researchers explain to the less learned that it is the wondrous spell of solar winds, funneling motes of sunfire into the earth's magnetic field. The journalists quiet beneath its display. The aurora always inspires reverence and humility. Inuit people in Greenland claim that their ancestors float in the aurora, playing football with the skull of a walrus. The Sami in Scandinavia tell a story about a proud boy who chose to mock the lights, skipping about the snow in a felt cap with his tongue out; the next morning, all that remained of him was a pile of ash. There are no tales about the lights here in the south, which is populated only by empires of penguins and the occasional stranded scientist, scooping peaches out of a can.

The captain slips in and out of lucidity. His scans are inconclusive, but the doctors fear the worst. They struggle to find a way to evacuate him to a real hospital. Katabatic winds make helicopter rescue impossible, and other ships, trying other angles of approach, also founder in the ice. On the few occasions that the captain sits up awake, he thirsts for the spray and open surge of the sea. Half sleeping, he imagines a stream of captains flowing through his room, men from around the world come to commiserate with their fellow man.

In the haze of his condition, he only vaguely understands that numerous icebreakers—many more than just his, the Chinese, and the Australian—are now trapped. The sea ice has spread beyond the expectations of scientists, beyond the wisdom of sailors. Few visitors can get to the Chinese ship wreathed in vicious glacial winds. Helicopters cower beneath their tarps. Some crews battle the elements to reach one another. Swedish sailors ski through the haze to a Japanese vessel. A Chilean crew wakes up one morning to find South Africans knocking on their hull. Tenuous lines of exchange form on the sea ice, sashimi traded for schnapps, red wine for dried sausage.

A dogsled team from a Canadian ship manages to make it to the Chinese boat. Snapping at their tethers, the huskies quicken as they near, licked by the aroma of pig innards stewed in garlic and oregano (the Filipino cook has run out of his more choice cuts of meat). On board, the Canadians find a chapped crew, blinking in the long daylight, the journalists tapping blearily at their screens, the researchers numb to ice, and the Russian captain asleep in his cot, his lungs moored to a pumping machine.

The last icebreaker reaches the Antarctic. It ponders a sad diorama, other icebreakers frozen in a shrinking chain to the horizon, all tilting to one side like sleeping tramps. (This is a lesson, its captain thinks, never be on time.) The ship sounds its foghorn. People spill out from the trapped ships, little black clumps flippering on the ice. The photographer takes out her telescopic lens and tries to shoot the icebreaker as it nuzzles the continent, as chunks of blue light fall away and the ice crackles. She clicks and clicks, but realizes that her camera is out of battery. Whether the last icebreaker succeeds or fails, she will not be able to record its progress.

Somewhere in the white beyond is the original cause, the Russian boat, the prisoner that summoned the others to become prisoners. Its skeletal crew huddle in the auditorium, eating rusks. They have watched the same Bollywood films over and over again. It feels to them that they have been counting their fingers and melting snow for weeks, or for years, or ever since they were born. Drunk under the aurora one night, the communications officer and the first mate go out onto the frozen deck and dance like lovers from another country.

ACKNOWLEDGMENTS

I can't help but feel that the writing of my first book was the work of many hands and minds beyond my own. Chief thanks go to my mother and my father, who submerged my upbringing in books, and to my twin brother, Ishaan, a constant support ever since he led me out into the world. I'm grateful as well to my grandparents, my uncles, my aunts, and all my cousins for their indulgence, storytelling, and affection. I'm lucky for all the teachers who have guided my imagination and craft, including Hilary Ainger, Geoffrey Worrell, Mridu Rai, Stefano Pello, Chuck Wachtel, and Jonathan Safran Foer. Thanks to David Godwin, Edward Orloff, and Mary Evans for shepherding my work into the light. Thanks to David Davidar, Ravi Mirchandani, Eric Chinski, Laird Gallagher, Simar Puneet, and all the wonderful staff at Aleph, FSG, and Picador. Thanks to Amitav Ghosh, Maryam Maruf, and Matthew Rohde for their encouragement and for reading these stories. Thanks to the NYU Creative Writing Program and the Millay Colony for supporting my work and giving me the space and time to become a better writer. And boundless thanks to Amanda, my wife, my reader, my wonder, my joy.